The Hacker's Heart

Table of Contents

Introduction 2
Chapter 1: The Code of Desire 5
Chapter 2: Unraveling Secrets 8
Chapter 3: Midnight Confessions 14
Chapter 4: The Pulse of Passion 21
Chapter 5: Lines of Seduction 26
Chapter 6: The Glitch in Love 32
Chapter 7: Firewalls and Flames 39
Chapter 8: Encrypted Emotions 48
Chapter 9: The Network of Trust 55
Chapter 10: Hacked by Love 63
Chapter 11: The Algorithm of Attraction 74
Chapter 12: Dangerous Desires 84
Chapter 13: The Virus of Lust 91
Chapter 14: Rebooting Romance 97
Chapter 15: The Encryption of Freedom 104

Introduction

The Hacker's Heart is a tantalizing blend of technology, passion, and the complexities of human emotion. Set against the backdrop of a world where code is king, and every keystroke can mean the difference between success and failure, this novel delves deep into the intertwined lives of those who navigate the digital frontier and the emotions that drive them.

The protagonist, Devon "Dev" Carter, is a brilliant but emotionally guarded African American hacker who has made a name for himself in the underground tech world. Known for his unmatched skills in breaking through the most complex security systems, Dev has built walls not only around the networks he invades but also around his own heart. His world is one of precision, logic, and control—until he encounters Jasmine "Jazz" Roberts, a fierce, independent woman who challenges his every preconception.

Jazz, a cybersecurity expert with a troubled past, is everything Dev isn't—open, passionate, and deeply connected to her emotions. Her beauty and intelligence captivate him, drawing him into a web of desire and vulnerability that he has spent years avoiding. But Jazz is more than just a pretty face; she's a formidable force in the tech world, with a reputation for exposing corruption and protecting the innocent. Her work has made her many enemies, some of whom are willing to do anything to take her down.

As Dev and Jazz's worlds collide, they find themselves entangled in a high-stakes game of cat and mouse. Their connection is instant and electric, a spark that quickly ignites into a blazing inferno of passion. But as they delve deeper into each other's lives, they uncover secrets that threaten to tear them apart. Dev's past is shrouded in mystery, filled with choices that haunt him, while Jazz's quest for justice puts them both in the crosshairs of powerful adversaries.

The Hacker's Heart is more than just a love story; it's a journey of self-discovery and redemption. It's about breaking down the barriers we create around ourselves, whether they're built from fear, pain, or past mistakes. As Dev and Jazz navigate the treacherous waters of their relationship, they must learn to trust each other—and themselves—if they hope to find true happiness.

This novel explores the intersection of technology and intimacy, examining how the digital age shapes our relationships and the ways we connect with others. It delves into themes of identity, power, and the ethics of hacking, all while maintaining a pulse-pounding narrative that will keep readers on the edge of their seats.

With its rich character development, sizzling romance, and thrilling plot twists, The Hacker's Heart is a story that will resonate with readers long after they turn the final page. It's a celebration of love in all its forms—the kind that burns bright, consumes you whole, and ultimately, leaves you changed forever.

Chapter 1: The Code of Desire

Devon "Dev" Carter sat in the dim glow of his dual monitors, his fingers dancing across the keyboard in a well-practiced rhythm. The room around him was silent, save for the occasional hum of the computer's fan and the click of keys. Lines of code scrolled rapidly across the screen, a digital symphony that only he could understand. This was his domain, a world where logic ruled and emotions were nothing more than distractions.

But tonight was different. Tonight, his focus was fractured, his mind drifting to thoughts that had nothing to do with the task at hand. It had been weeks since he first crossed paths with Jasmine "Jazz" Roberts, but her image was as clear in his mind as if she were standing right in front of him. Her smile, her confidence, the way she seemed to see right through him—it all lingered, a constant, unwanted presence in his thoughts.

Dev had never been one to let emotions get in the way of his work. His reputation as one of the best hackers in the underground world was built on his ability to stay detached, to view every job as a puzzle to be solved, nothing more. But Jazz had shaken that foundation. She was different from anyone he'd ever met—strong, intelligent, and unafraid to challenge him. Their encounters had left him both intrigued and unsettled, stirring feelings he hadn't experienced in years.

As he continued to work, his thoughts kept drifting back to their last conversation. It had been brief, a chance meeting at a tech conference where they had exchanged only a few words. But those words had stuck with him, echoing in his mind like a melody he couldn't shake. She had mentioned a new project she was working on, something big, something dangerous. And despite himself, Dev found that he wanted to know more.

He shook his head, trying to refocus on the code in front of him. Emotions were a liability, a weakness that could be exploited. He couldn't afford to let his guard down, not now, not ever. But as much as he tried to push her out of his mind, she kept slipping back in, like a virus that had wormed its way into his system.

With a frustrated sigh, Dev leaned back in his chair and rubbed his temples. He needed to get a grip, to compartmentalize, the way he always did. Jazz was just a distraction, nothing more. But deep down, he knew that wasn't true. There was something about her, something that pulled at him in a way he couldn't ignore.

He glanced at the clock on the screen. It was late, but he wasn't tired. If anything, he felt more awake, more alive than he had in a long time. Maybe it was the thrill of the chase, the challenge of trying to figure her out. Or maybe it was something else, something he wasn't ready to admit.

Before he could overthink it, he pushed himself away from the desk and grabbed his jacket. He needed air, a break from the suffocating confines of his apartment. As he stepped out into the cool night, he felt a strange sense of anticipation, as if something was about to change.

And in the back of his mind, a voice whispered that maybe, just maybe, it was time to stop running from his feelings and start facing them head-on.

The remaining chapters will follow the progression of Dev and Jazz's relationship, delving into their personal struggles, the dangers they face, and the passion that threatens to consume them both. Each chapter will build upon the tension and chemistry between the characters, leading to a climax that is as explosive as it is satisfying.

Chapter 2: Unraveling Secrets

The city lights flickered like a thousand digital codes, each one revealing a fragment of the truth. Devon Carter walked through the crowded streets, his thoughts miles away from the bustling nightlife around him. The cold night air did little to clear his mind; instead, it seemed to amplify the confusion that Jazz had stirred within him. He had never been one to let a woman get under his skin, but there was something about her—something he couldn't shake.

Dev had always been a man of secrets. He knew how to hide in the shadows, how to slip through the cracks of society without leaving a trace. His hacking skills had made him a ghost in the digital world, but in the real world, he was just as elusive. Few people knew the real Dev Carter, and even fewer had been close enough to scratch the surface. But Jazz had done more than that. She had struck something deep within him, something he had buried long ago.

He found himself standing in front of a nondescript building, its facade blending in with the surrounding structures. The sign above the door was faded, barely legible, but Dev knew this place well. It was a hacker's haven, a place where people like him could find work, information, or simply disappear. Inside, the air was thick with the hum of computers and the low murmur of voices. He had come here countless times before, but tonight felt different.

As he pushed open the door and stepped inside, he was greeted by the familiar sights and sounds of the underground tech world. The room was dimly lit, with rows of computers lining the walls. A few figures sat hunched over their screens, their faces illuminated by the glow of monitors. In the corner, a man with a thick beard and a hooded sweatshirt looked up from his work, his eyes narrowing as he recognized Dev.

"Carter," the man said, his voice gruff. "Long time, no see. What brings you here?"

"Need some information, Marcus," Dev replied, his tone casual but firm. He knew Marcus well—an old contact who specialized in digging up dirt on.anyone and anything. If there was something to know, Marcus could find it.

Marcus raised an eyebrow, clearly intrigued. "Information, huh? That's not like you. What's on your mind?"

"Someone," Dev said, leaning against the counter. "I need everything you can find on Jasmine Roberts."

Marcus's expression shifted, a mix of curiosity and caution. "Roberts? The cybersecurity expert? She's pretty high profile, Carter. What's your interest in her?"

"That's my business," Dev said, his voice leaving no room for argument. "Can you do it or not?"

Marcus shrugged. "Of course I can. But it'll cost you. She's got a lot of eyes on her, and digging too deep might stir up trouble."

Dev reached into his pocket and pulled out a small stack of cash, sliding it across the counter. "This should cover it. I need everything—her background, her connections, any enemies she might have made."

Marcus took the money, his fingers deftly counting the bills before he slipped them into his pocket. "Give me a couple of days. I'll see what I can dig up. But be careful, Carter. Roberts isn't someone you want to mess with."

"I'll take my chances," Dev said, his mind already racing with the possibilities. He turned to leave, but Marcus's voice stopped him.

"Hey, Carter," Marcus called out. "Why her? What's so special about Jasmine Roberts?"

Dev paused, his hand on the door. For a moment, he considered telling Marcus the truth—that he wasn't entirely sure why he was so drawn to Jazz, that something about her had ignited a fire within him that he couldn't extinguish. But instead, he simply said, "She's a puzzle I need to solve."

And with that, he stepped back into the night, leaving Marcus to wonder what kind of game Devon Carter was playing.

The next few days passed in a blur of anticipation and unease. Dev threw himself into his work, trying to distract himself from the growing obsession that Jazz had become. But no matter how hard he tried, he couldn't shake the feeling that he was getting in over his head.

Late one evening, just as he was about to call it a night, his phone buzzed with a message. It was from Marcus.

"Got what you asked for. Meet me at the usual place."

Dev's heart quickened as he grabbed his jacket and headed out the door. The "usual place" was a small, out-of-the-way café that catered to people like him—those who valued privacy and discretion. When he arrived, Marcus was already there, a manila envelope sitting on the table in front of him.

"Here's everything I could find," Marcus said, sliding the envelope toward Dev as he sat down. "You were right—she's got a lot of skeletons in her closet."

Dev took the envelope, his fingers hesitating for just a moment before he opened it. Inside was a thick stack of papers, each one detailing a different aspect of Jazz's life. There were copies of old school records, employment histories, and even a few photos from her past. But as he flipped through the pages, one thing became clear—Jazz was more than just a cybersecurity expert. She had a past that was just as complicated, just as shadowed as his own.

One document in particular caught his eye—a police report from several years ago, detailing an incident that had nearly cost Jazz her life. According to the report, she had been involved in a high-profile case against a major tech corporation, exposing their illegal activities to the public. The fallout had been severe, with Jazz narrowly escaping an attempt on her life.

Dev felt a chill run down his spine as he read the report. Jazz had enemies—powerful ones. And now that he was getting closer to her, those enemies might become his as well.

But as much as the information disturbed him, it also made him more determined than ever to protect her. He knew what it was like to live in the shadows, to be constantly looking over your shoulder. And he couldn't stand the thought of Jazz facing that danger alone.

"Thanks, Marcus," Dev said, slipping the envelope into his jacket. "You've been a big help."

Marcus nodded, but his expression was serious. "Watch your back, Carter. You're playing a dangerous game."

Dev knew Marcus was right. But he couldn't stop now. He had to see this through, had to unravel the secrets that Jazz was hiding—and maybe, just maybe, find a way to let her into his guarded heart.

As he left the café and walked into the night, Dev couldn't help but feel that he was on the brink of something big, something that would change everything. He didn't know where this path would lead, but one thing was certain—he was no longer just a hacker lost in his own world. He was a man who had found something worth fighting for.

And he would do whatever it took to protect her, even if it meant risking everything.

Chapter 3: Midnight Confessions

The following night was quieter than usual. Devon Carter sat at his desk, the glow of the monitors casting long shadows across the room. His apartment, once a haven of solitude and control, now felt like a cage. The walls seemed to close in on him as the weight of what he had learned about Jazz pressed down on his chest. He couldn't stop thinking about the police report, the danger she had faced, and the enemies she had made along the way. It was all too familiar, like staring into a dark mirror of his own life.

He had always been good at compartmentalizing his emotions, tucking them away in a box labeled "unimportant." But Jazz had shattered that box, scattering the contents all over his carefully ordered life. She was different from anyone he had ever met—strong, intelligent, fearless—and yet, she carried a vulnerability that he couldn't ignore. She had been through hell, just like him, and it only made him more determined to protect her, no matter the cost.

Dev's thoughts were interrupted by the sound of his phone buzzing on the desk. He glanced at the screen and saw Jazz's name flash across it. For a moment, he hesitated, his thumb hovering over the answer button. He wasn't sure he was ready to talk to her, not after everything he had learned. But he knew he couldn't avoid her forever.

"Hey, Jazz," he said, trying to keep his voice steady as he answered the call.

"Hey, Dev," she replied, her voice soft but tinged with something he couldn't quite place—was it worry? Or maybe something else, something deeper. "Are you busy?"

"Not really. Just... working on some stuff. What's up?"

"I was wondering if you wanted to meet up tonight. I know it's late, but there's something I need to talk to you about."

Dev's heart skipped a beat. He could tell from her tone that this wasn't just a casual request. There was something serious on her mind, something she wasn't sure how to say over the phone.

"Sure," he said, trying to sound casual even though his mind was racing. "Where do you want to meet?"

"There's a park near my place," Jazz said. "It's quiet at this time of night, and we won't be disturbed. I'll text you the address."

"Okay, I'll be there in twenty."

As he hung up the phone, Dev felt a knot tighten in his stomach. He didn't know what Jazz wanted to talk about, but he had a feeling it wasn't going to be easy. He grabbed his jacket and headed out the door, his mind running through a thousand possibilities of what she might say.

The park was only a short drive away, nestled in a quiet neighborhood where the city's noise seemed to fade into the background. As he pulled up and parked, he saw Jazz standing near a small grove of trees, her silhouette outlined by the soft glow of a nearby streetlamp. She looked beautiful, but there was a tension in her posture that told him she was on edge.

Dev approached her quietly, his footsteps muffled by the soft grass. "Hey," he said as he reached her, trying to gauge her mood. "What's going on?"

Jazz turned to face him, her eyes searching his as if trying to find the right words. For a moment, she seemed to hesitate, and Dev could see the battle going on inside her. Then, she took a deep breath and spoke.

"There's something you need to know, Dev," she said, her voice steady but laced with emotion. "Something I haven't told you."

Dev's heart pounded in his chest. He had been prepared for this, or at least he thought he had. But hearing the uncertainty in her voice made him realize just how much this conversation meant to her.

"Whatever it is, you can tell me," he said, his voice soft but firm. "I'm here for you, Jazz."

She nodded, her gaze dropping to the ground for a moment before she looked back up at him. "I've... I've been involved in some pretty dangerous stuff over the years," she began, her voice trembling slightly. "I'm not just a cybersecurity expert, Dev. I've taken on some of the biggest corporations out there—exposing corruption, bringing down criminals who think they're untouchable. But it's cost me."

Dev listened intently, his mind flashing back to the police report, the near-fatal incident that had almost taken her life. He had known she was involved in something big, but hearing it from her own lips made it all the more real.

"I knew you were involved in some high-stakes stuff," Dev said, choosing his words carefully. "But I didn't realize how deep it went."

Jazz's eyes glistened with unshed tears, but she didn't let them fall. "I've made enemies, Dev. Powerful enemies. And they've been after me for years. I've been able to stay one step ahead of them, but... it's only a matter of time before they catch up."

Dev felt a surge of protectiveness rise within him. He wanted to reach out, to pull her into his arms and promise her that everything would be okay. But he knew that wouldn't be enough. She needed more than just words; she needed someone who understood, someone who could help her fight back.

"I'm not going to let that happen," Dev said, his voice low but fierce. "You don't have to do this alone, Jazz. I've got your back."

Jazz looked at him, her eyes searching his for any sign of doubt. But all she saw was determination and something else—something that made her heart skip a beat. She had been strong for so long, had fought so many battles on her own, that she had forgotten what it felt like to have someone by her side.

"Why are you doing this, Dev?" she asked, her voice barely above a whisper. "Why do you care so much?"

Dev hesitated, the words he wanted to say caught in his throat. He had never been good at expressing his feelings, at letting people in. But with Jazz, it was different. She made him want to be honest, to be vulnerable in a way he hadn't been in years.

"Because you're worth it," he finally said, his voice rough with emotion. "Because you're the first person who's made me feel alive in a long time. And because I can't stand the thought of losing you."

Jazz's breath caught in her throat as she heard his words. For a moment, she didn't know what to say, didn't know how to respond to the raw honesty in his voice. But then she realized that she didn't need to say anything. She stepped closer to him, her hand reaching out to touch his.

Their fingers intertwined, and for a moment, they just stood there, letting the connection between them speak louder than words ever could. Dev could feel the warmth of her hand, the steady beat of her pulse against his skin, and he knew that he was falling for her—falling hard.

"I'm scared, Dev," Jazz whispered, her voice trembling. "I've been running for so long, and I don't know how to stop."

"You don't have to run anymore," Dev said, his voice firm and reassuring. "We'll face this together, whatever comes our way. I'm not going anywhere."

Jazz looked up at him, her eyes filled with a mix of fear and hope. For the first time in a long time, she allowed herself to believe that maybe, just maybe, she didn't have to do this alone. Maybe she could let someone in, let Dev in, and together they could face whatever the future held.

Without thinking, she leaned in, her lips brushing against his in a tentative kiss. It was soft at first, a gentle exploration of something new and uncertain. But as the seconds passed, the kiss deepened, fueled by the unspoken emotions that had been building between them for so long.

Dev's arms wrapped around her, pulling her closer as he lost himself in the taste of her lips, the feel of her body against his. For the first time in years, he let go of the control he had always clung to, surrendering to the emotions that had been simmering beneath the surface.

When they finally pulled apart, both of them were breathless, their hearts racing in sync. Jazz looked up at him, her eyes bright with something that looked a lot like love.

"Thank you, Dev," she whispered, her voice filled with gratitude and something deeper. "For everything."

"You don't have to thank me," Dev said, his voice soft but filled with conviction. "Just promise me one thing."

"What's that?" Jazz asked, her heart pounding in her chest.

"Promise me you'll trust me," Dev said, his eyes locking onto hers. "Promise me you'll let me in."

Jazz felt the weight of his words, the vulnerability they held. It was a promise she had never made to anyone, a leap of faith that scared her more than anything else. But as she looked into his eyes, she knew that she could make that promise, that she wanted to make that promise.

"I promise," she said, her voice steady despite the fear that still lingered in the back of her mind. "I'll trust you, Dev. I'll let you in."

And with those words, a new chapter began in their lives—one filled with uncertainty, danger, and a love that had the power to break down even the strongest of walls.

Chapter 4: The Pulse of Passion

The days that followed were a whirlwind of emotions, secrecy, and stolen moments. Devon and Jazz found themselves navigating the complexities of their newfound relationship, trying to balance the passion that had ignited between them with the very real dangers that lurked in the shadows. The intensity of their connection was both exhilarating and terrifying, a force that neither of them had anticipated but neither could deny.

Dev had never been one to let his guard down, but with Jazz, it was different. She had a way of making him feel things he had long buried, emotions he thought he had locked away for good. He found himself drawn to her in ways that went beyond physical attraction. There was a depth to their connection that he hadn't experienced before, a sense of understanding and mutual respect that made him want to protect her at all costs.

But with that connection came vulnerability, and Dev wasn't used to feeling vulnerable. He was a man who thrived on control, who lived his life by a set of rules designed to keep him safe. Yet with Jazz, those rules seemed to blur, and he found himself questioning everything he thought he knew about love, trust, and loyalty.

Jazz, on the other hand, was struggling with her own fears. She had spent so much of her life fighting battles on her own, relying on no one but herself. Letting Dev into her life, into her heart, was both exhilarating and terrifying. She was used to being strong, to holding the weight of the world on her shoulders without flinching. But now, with Dev by her side, she was starting to realize that strength didn't have to mean solitude.

One evening, as the sun dipped below the horizon, casting a warm golden glow over the city, Dev found himself standing on the balcony of Jazz's apartment. The view from her place was stunning, the city spread out beneath them like a vast, glittering network of lights. But Dev's attention wasn't on the view; it was on Jazz, who stood beside him, her hand resting lightly on the railing as she gazed out at the city.

"You know," Jazz said softly, breaking the comfortable silence between them, "I've never really had someone to share this with. The view, the quiet moments… it's always been just me."

Dev turned to look at her, his heart tightening at the vulnerability in her voice. "You don't have to be alone anymore, Jazz," he said, his voice firm but gentle. "I'm here, and I'm not going anywhere."

Jazz smiled, though there was a hint of sadness in her eyes. "I want to believe that Dev. I really do. But part of me is still scared—scared that this is all too good to be true."

Dev reached out, his hand gently cupping her chin as he tilted her face up to meet his gaze. "It's not too good to be true," he said, his voice filled with conviction. "What we have is real, Jazz. And I'm going to do whatever it takes to prove that to you."

For a moment, they just looked at each other, the intensity of their emotions hanging in the air between them. Then, without a word, Dev leaned in, capturing her lips in a kiss that was both tender and demanding. Jazz responded immediately, her arms wrapping around his neck as she pressed herself against him, losing herself in the feel of his body against hers.

The kiss deepened, becoming more urgent as the passion between them flared to life. Dev's hands slid down her back, pulling her even closer as he tasted the sweetness of her lips, the warmth of her breath mingling with his. Every touch, every caress sent sparks of electricity through his body, igniting a fire that burned hotter with each passing second.

Jazz felt the same fire coursing through her veins, a heat that consumed her, making her forget everything but the man in her arms. She had never felt this way before—so alive, so connected to someone else. It was as if they were two halves of a whole, fitting together in a way that was both exhilarating and terrifying.

Without breaking the kiss, Dev guided her back inside the apartment, his hands never leaving her body as they moved toward the bedroom. The world outside faded away, leaving only the two of them, lost in the heat of their desire.

When they reached the bed, Dev paused, his breath coming in ragged gasps as he looked down at her. "Are you sure about this?" he asked, his voice hoarse with restraint. "I don't want to rush you."

Jazz looked up at him, her eyes dark with passion. "I've never been surer of anything in my life," she whispered, her hands sliding up his chest to rest on his shoulders. "I want this, Dev. I want you."

That was all the encouragement he needed. With a groan, Dev captured her lips in another searing kiss, his hands working quickly to remove the barriers between them. Clothes were discarded in a frenzy of need, and soon they were skin to skin, their bodies pressed together in a way that left no room for doubt.

The first touch of his skin against hers sent a shiver down Jazz's spine, a sensation that was both thrilling and comforting. She had never felt so connected to someone, so utterly in sync with their every movement, their every breath. It was as if they were two parts of a whole, finally coming together in a way that was both powerful and deeply satisfying.

Dev's hands moved over her body with a reverence that made her heart ache. He touched her as if she were something precious, something to be cherished and protected. And in that moment, Jazz knew that she had made the right choice in letting him into her life, into her heart.

As they came together, their bodies moving in perfect harmony, Jazz felt the last of her fears melt away. She wasn't alone anymore. She had Dev, and together, they could face whatever the world threw at them. Their passion was a force of nature, unstoppable and undeniable, and it left both of them breathless, lost in the ecstasy of the moment.

When it was over, they lay tangled together, their bodies still humming with the aftershocks of their passion. Dev held her close, his fingers tracing lazy patterns on her skin as they caught their breath. Jazz rested her head on his chest, listening to the steady rhythm of his heartbeat, a sound that was as comforting as it was grounding.

"I never thought I could feel like this," Jazz murmured, her voice barely above a whisper. "I never thought I could let someone in."

Dev tightened his hold on her, his lips brushing against the top of her head. "You don't have to be afraid anymore, Jazz," he said softly. "I'm here, and I'm not going anywhere."

For the first time in a long time, Jazz allowed herself to believe those words. She had spent so much of her life running, hiding, and fighting to survive. But now, with Dev by her side, she felt something she hadn't felt in years—hope.

As they drifted off to sleep, their bodies still entwined, both of them knew that the road ahead wouldn't be easy. There were still dangers lurking in the shadows, enemies waiting to strike. But for now, in this moment, they had each other. And that was enough.

Chapter 5: Lines of Seduction

The morning sunlight filtered through the curtains, casting a warm glow over the bedroom. Devon Carter lay awake, his eyes tracing the delicate curve of Jazz's shoulder as she slept peacefully beside him. The events of the night before played over in his mind like a well-loved record, each memory bringing a smile to his lips. It had been years since he had felt this content, this connected to another person. But even as he basked in the afterglow of their passion, a part of him couldn't shake the sense of foreboding that lingered in the back of his mind.

He knew their happiness was fragile, a delicate thing that could be shattered by the dangers that still loomed over them. Jazz's enemies were real, and they were powerful. The more time he spent with her, the more he realized just how deep the threat ran. But he also knew that walking away wasn't an option. He was in too deep, his heart too invested to turn back now.

Jazz stirred beside him, her eyelids fluttering open as she slowly woke up. When her eyes met his, a soft smile spread across her face, and she reached up to touch his cheek, her fingers tracing the line of his jaw.

"Good morning," she whispered, her voice still heavy with sleep.

"Good morning," Dev replied, leaning down to press a gentle kiss to her lips. "How are you feeling?"

"Happy," she said, her smile widening as she snuggled closer to him. "Content. Like I'm exactly where I'm supposed to be."

Dev's heart swelled at her words, but he couldn't ignore the nagging worry that tugged at his thoughts. "Jazz, there's something I need to talk to you about," he said, his voice serious.

Jazz immediately picked up on the shift in his tone, her smile fading as she pulled back slightly to look at him. "What is it?" she asked, concern creeping into her voice.

Dev hesitated for a moment, unsure of how to begin. But he knew that he couldn't keep his concerns from her, not when the stakes were so high. "I've been thinking a lot about what you told me—about your past, the enemies you've made," he began, his eyes searching hers. "I want to help you, Jazz. I want to make sure you're safe. But I need to know everything. I need to know what we're up against."

Jazz sighed, her expression softening as she realized where this conversation was headed. "I was afraid you'd say that" she admitted, her voice tinged with regret. "I didn't want to drag you into this, Dev. I wanted to protect you from the mess that my life has become."

"You don't have to protect me," Dev said firmly, taking her hand in his. "We're in this together now. Whatever it is, we'll face it side by side. But I need to know the truth, Jazz. All of it."

Jazz looked into his eyes, searching for any sign of doubt, any hesitation. But all she saw was the unwavering determination of a man who was willing to stand by her no matter what. It was a realization that both comforted and terrified her.

"Alright," she said finally, taking a deep breath. "I'll tell you everything."

They spent the next few hours talking, the morning giving way to afternoon as Jazz recounted the details of her past. She told him about the corporations she had exposed, the criminals she had brought to justice, and the powerful enemies she had made along the way. She spoke of the near-fatal incident that had forced her into hiding, the constant fear that had become a part of her everyday life. And as she spoke, Dev listened intently, piecing together the puzzle of her life with a growing sense of resolve.

"It's worse than I thought," Dev said quietly when she had finished, his mind racing with the implications of what he had learned. "These people... they won't stop until they've silenced you for good."

"I know," Jazz replied, her voice heavy with resignation. "That's why I've been so careful, why I've kept so much to myself. But no matter how hard I try to stay ahead of them, they always seem to be one step behind."

Dev's jaw clenched, his hands tightening into fists as he thought about the dangers she had been facing alone. "Not anymore," he said, his voice filled with determination. "I won't let them hurt you, Jazz. We'll find a way to take them down, to make sure they can't come after you again."

Jazz looked at him, a mixture of hope and fear in her eyes. "How, Dev? These people are untouchable. They have resources, connections... they're playing a game we can't win."

Dev shook his head, a fierce light in his eyes. "They might think they're untouchable, but everyone has a weakness. We just need to find it. And I have a few ideas on where to start."

Jazz raised an eyebrow, her curiosity piqued. "Oh? And what exactly do you have in mind?"

"I've been doing some digging of my own," Dev said, his voice lowering as he leaned in closer. "There's a hacker I know—someone who specializes in exposing secrets, finding information that others want to keep hidden. If anyone can help us, it's him. But it won't be easy. He's a ghost, even in the hacking community. It'll take some time to track him down."

Jazz nodded, her mind racing as she considered the possibilities. "And once we find him?"

"Once we find him, we get him on our side," Dev replied. "We use his skills to expose the people who are after you, to turn the tables on them. If we can gather enough evidence, we can bring them down for good."

Jazz's eyes widened as she realized the scope of what Dev was proposing. It was a dangerous plan, one that would require both of them to take risks they had never taken before. But it was also a chance to finally put an end to the nightmare she had been living.

"Do you really think it could work?" she asked, her voice barely above a whisper.

Dev reached out, taking her hand in his and giving it a reassuring squeeze. "I do," he said, his voice filled with conviction. "But we have to be smart about this. We can't rush in without a plan. We need to be patient, to play the long game. But I promise you, Jazz—we will win."

Jazz felt a surge of hope at his words, a flicker of light in the darkness that had surrounded her for so long. For the first time in years, she allowed herself to believe that there was a way out, that she could finally be free of the past that had haunted her.

"I trust you, Dev," she said, her voice steady despite the emotions swirling within her. "Whatever it takes, I'm with you."

Dev smiled, leaning in to press a gentle kiss to her forehead. "We'll get through this, Jazz. Together."

As the afternoon sun streamed through the windows, casting a golden light over the room, the two of them sat in silence, their hands entwined as they stared out at the city beyond.

The road ahead was uncertain, filled with dangers and challenges they couldn't yet foresee. But with each other by their side, they knew they could face whatever came their way.

And so, as they prepared to embark on a journey that would test their strength, their courage, and their love, they found solace in the one thing that had brought them together in the first place—a deep, unshakable connection that no one could ever take away.

Chapter 6: The Glitch in Love

The following days passed in a blur of planning and preparation. Devon and Jazz spent countless hours strategizing, gathering information, and piecing together the complex web of connections that linked her enemies. The more they uncovered, the more dangerous the situation became, but neither of them was willing to back down. They had come too far, and the stakes were too high.

Dev was meticulous in his approach, carefully mapping out every possible angle, every potential threat. He knew that one wrong move could put Jazz's life in even greater danger, and the thought of losing her was something he couldn't bear. Jazz, for her part, was just as determined. She was tired of living in fear, of constantly looking over her shoulder. This was her chance to take control of her life again, and she was ready to do whatever it took.

Despite the seriousness of their mission, there were moments of tenderness and connection that helped to sustain them. Late at night, after hours of intense work, they would find solace in each other's arms, their passion a reminder of the bond that had brought them together. In those quiet moments, they could forget about the dangers they faced, if only for a little while.

One evening, as they sat in Devon's apartment surrounded by papers, laptops, and empty coffee cups, Jazz leaned back in her chair, rubbing her temples. "This is like trying to solve a puzzle with half the pieces missing," she said, frustration evident in her voice. "Every time we think we're getting closer, something else pops up."

Dev looked over at her, concern etched on his face. "We're making progress, Jazz. It might not feel like it, but we are. We've already identified a few key players, and once we have enough evidence, we can move on to the next phase."

Jazz sighed, her fingers tapping restlessly on the table. "I know. It's just... I wish there was a way to speed this up. The longer we take, the more dangerous it becomes."

Dev reached out, placing his hand over hers. "I get it. But we have to be careful. Rushing in without all the facts could get us both killed. We'll get there, I promise."

Jazz nodded, appreciating his calm reassurance. But beneath the surface, her frustration and anxiety were growing. She had always been a woman of action, someone who didn't shy away from a challenge. But this waiting, this feeling of being one step behind, was wearing on her.

That night, after Jazz had fallen asleep in his bed, Dev sat at his computer, the soft glow of the screen illuminating his face. He was going over the latest data they had gathered, trying to find a pattern, a clue that would give them the breakthrough they needed. But as the hours ticked by, his eyes grew heavy, and his focus began to waver.

He was just about to call it a night when a message popped up on his screen. It was from an anonymous source, the sender's identity hidden behind layers of encryption. Dev's heart skipped a beat as he opened the message, his instincts telling him that this could be important.

The message was short, just a few lines of text, but it was enough to send a chill down his spine.

You're getting too close. Back off, or she pays the price.

Dev's blood ran cold as he stared at the screen, his mind racing. Whoever had sent the message knew exactly what they were doing. This wasn't just a threat—it was a warning. A warning that they were being watched that every move they made was being monitored.

Without thinking, Dev jumped out of his chair and rushed to the bedroom, his heart pounding in his chest. Jazz was still asleep, her breathing steady and peaceful, unaware of the danger that loomed over them. Dev stood in the doorway, his fists clenched, his mind a whirlwind of emotions. He had promised to protect her, to keep her safe, but now it felt like the walls were closing in.

He knew what he had to do. They needed to be even more cautious, more vigilant. But most of all, he needed to find out who was behind the message and why they were targeting Jazz. This was no longer just about gathering information—it was about survival.

The next morning, as they sat together over breakfast, Dev decided to tell Jazz about the message. He knew she deserved to know, and that keeping it from her would only make things worse in the long run.

"Jazz," he began, his voice steady but serious, "something happened last night. I got a message… a threat, actually. Someone's watching us. They know we're getting close."

Jazz looked up from her coffee, her eyes wide with concern. "A threat? What did it say?"

Dev recounted the message, watching her reaction carefully. He could see the worry in her eyes, but there was also a spark of determination, a fire that told him she wasn't going to back down.

"So, they're scared," she said, her voice resolute. "They wouldn't be threatening us if we weren't on the right track."

"Maybe," Dev agreed. "But it also means we have to be even more careful. We can't afford any mistakes. Whoever this is, they're serious, and they're not afraid to hurt you to get what they want."

Jazz reached across the table, taking his hand in hers. "We'll figure this out, Dev. Together. I'm not going to let them win."

Dev squeezed her hand, a sense of pride swelling in his chest. Jazz was strong—stronger than anyone he had ever known. But he also knew that strength alone wouldn't be enough to keep them safe. They needed a plan, and they needed it fast.

Over the next few days, they doubled their efforts, working tirelessly to track down the source of the message. Dev reached out to his contacts in the hacking community, calling in favors and following every lead, no matter how small. Jazz used her own network of connections, tapping into resources she hadn't used in years.

It was exhausting work, but neither of them was willing to give up. They were fueled by a shared sense of purpose, a determination to see this through to the end. But as the days turned into nights and the pressure mounted, the cracks in their resolve began to show.

One evening, after another long day of chasing down dead ends, Jazz finally reached her breaking point. They were sitting in the living room, surrounded by papers and laptops, when she suddenly stood up, her hands clenched into fists.

"This is getting us nowhere!" she exclaimed, her voice rising in frustration. "We're spinning our wheels, and they're out there, watching us, waiting for us to make a mistake. I can't stand this, Dev. I can't stand feeling so powerless!"

Dev looked up at her, his heart aching at the sight of her frustration. He understood her anger, her need to take action, but he also knew that acting rashly could put them both in even greater danger.

"I know it's hard, Jazz," he said, his voice calm but firm. "But we have to be patient. We can't afford to make any mistakes right now. We're close, I can feel it. We just need to keep going."

Jazz shook her head, her eyes filled with a mix of anger and despair. "I'm tired of being patient, Dev. I'm tired of waiting for something to happen. I want to fight back, to take control again!"

Dev stood up, crossing the room to stand in front of her. He reached out, gently cupping her face in his hands, forcing her to look at him. "You are in control, Jazz," he said softly. "You've been fighting your whole life, and you've survived things that would break most people. But right now, the best way to fight is to be smart, to be careful. We're going to get through this, I promise you. But we have to do it together."

Jazz stared up at him, her breath coming in shallow gasps as she fought to keep her emotions in check. She knew he was right—knew that they couldn't afford to let their guard down. But the fear, the frustration, the anger—it was all becoming too much to bear.

"I just... I don't know how much more of this I can take," she admitted, her voice trembling with emotion.

Dev pulled her into his arms, holding her close as he whispered soothing words into her ear. "You're not alone, Jazz," he murmured, his voice steady and reassuring. "I'm here, and I'm not going anywhere. We'll get through this, I promise you. Just hold on a little longer."

Jazz buried her face in his chest, her arms wrapping around him as she clung to the comfort of his embrace. In that moment, she realized just how much she had come to rely on him, how deeply she had fallen for the man who had entered her life so unexpectedly. He was her rock, her anchor in the storm that threatened to consume them both.

As they stood there, wrapped in each other's arms, Jazz knew that no matter what happened, no matter how dark the road ahead might be, she could face it as long as Dev was by her side. Together, they were stronger than the fear, stronger than the threats that loomed over them. And together, they would find a way to win.

But as the days wore on and the tension between them grew, Jazz couldn't shake the feeling that something was about to go wrong. There was a glitch in the code of their plan, a flaw that neither of them could see. And when that glitch revealed itself, it would test the limits of their love, their trust, and their resolve in ways they had never imagined.

Chapter 7: Firewalls and Flames

As the days stretched into weeks, the tension between Devon and Jazz became palpable, an invisible force that seemed to follow them everywhere. The constant stress of their situation weighed heavily on both of them, eroding the sense of security they had built together. Despite their best efforts, the leads they followed often ended in dead ends, and the few breakthroughs they had were met with new challenges that only deepened the complexity of their mission.

Dev found himself increasingly on edge, his mind constantly racing with thoughts of how to protect Jazz and stay one step ahead of her enemies. The sleepless nights spent scouring the dark web for clues, the endless hours spent analyzing data and tracking down leads—it was all starting to take its toll. His normally sharp mind was clouded with exhaustion, and the weight of responsibility pressed down on him like a heavy burden.

Jazz, too, was struggling. The fear that had once driven her to fight back now threatened to consume her, and the frustration of their stalled progress only added to her anxiety. She had always prided herself on being strong, on facing challenges head-on, but the endless cycle of threats and uncertainty was wearing her down. She began to withdraw, retreating into herself as the pressure mounted.

Their relationship, once a source of comfort and strength, was now strained under the weight of their circumstances. The passion that had once burned so brightly between them was now flickering like a dying flame, overshadowed by the fear and frustration that loomed over them. They still loved each other deeply, but the situation they found themselves in was testing the limits of that love.

One evening, after another day of fruitless searching and dead-end leads, the tension between them finally reached its breaking point. They were in Devon's apartment, the room dimly lit by the soft glow of the computer screens. Jazz was pacing back and forth, her frustration evident in every step, while Dev sat at his desk, his eyes glued to the screen in front of him.

"This isn't working, Dev," Jazz said, her voice sharp with frustration. "We're getting nowhere. Every lead we follow just brings us back to the same place—nowhere. We're running in circles, and it's driving me crazy!"

Dev didn't look up from the screen, his fingers typing furiously as he tried to track down yet another lead. "I know it's frustrating, Jazz," he said, his voice tired but calm. "But we have to keep going. We're close, I can feel it. We just need to be patient."

"Patient?" Jazz snapped, stopping in her tracks to glare at him. "We've been patient, Dev! We've been patient for weeks, and what do we have to show for it? Nothing! I'm tired of waiting for something to happen. I want to take action, to fight back!"

Dev finally looked up from the screen, his eyes meeting hers with a mixture of concern and irritation. "I get it, Jazz. I really do. But rushing in without a plan isn't going to help us. We have to be smart about this. We can't afford any mistakes."

Jazz threw her hands up in frustration. "That's all you ever say! 'We have to be smart,' 'We have to be patient.' But while we're sitting here playing it safe, they're out there, watching us, waiting for the perfect moment to strike. I can't just sit here and do nothing, Dev. I need to do something!"

Dev's patience finally snapped. He stood up, his voice rising in frustration. "And what do you suggest we do, Jazz? Charge in guns blazing? That's exactly what they want! They're counting on us to make a mistake, to get desperate. We can't give them that satisfaction!"

Jazz's eyes flashed with anger; her hands clenched into fists at her sides. "You don't get it, do you? This isn't just some game, Dev! This is my life! I'm the one they're after, the one they want to hurt. I can't just sit here and wait for them to come to me. I have to fight back, or I'll lose everything!"

Dev took a step closer to her, his voice low and intense. "And you think I don't know that? You think I'm not doing everything I can to keep you safe? I've been fighting just as hard as you have, Jazz. But we have to do this the right way, or we'll lose everything."

Jazz's anger suddenly gave way to a wave of emotion, her eyes filling with tears as she looked at him. "I'm scared, Dev," she admitted, her voice trembling. "I'm scared that if we keep waiting, it'll be too late. I'm scared that I'll lose you, that I'll lose everything we've built together. I can't go through that again."

Dev's heart softened at her words, the anger and frustration melting away as he reached out to pull her into his arms. "You're not going to lose me, Jazz," he said, his voice filled with reassurance. "I'm here, and I'm not going anywhere. We're going to get through this, I promise you. But we have to stay strong. We can't let them win."

Jazz buried her face in his chest, her tears soaking into his shirt as she clung to him. "I just want this to be over," she whispered, her voice choked with emotion. "I just want to feel safe again."

Dev held her close, his hand gently stroking her hair as he whispered soothing words into her ear. "We'll get there, Jazz. We'll find a way to make this right. But we have to stay focused. We can't let the fear control us."

They stood there for a long time, wrapped in each other's arms, finding solace in the connection that had brought them together. Despite the fear, the frustration, and the uncertainty that surrounded them, they knew that they could face anything as long as they had each other.

As the tension between them eased, Dev gently guided Jazz over to the couch, where they sat down together. He held her close, his arms wrapped around her as they both took a moment to breathe, to regroup. The road ahead was still uncertain, but they knew that they had to face it together, as a team.

After a few moments of silence, Dev spoke again, his voice calm and thoughtful. "There's something I've been thinking about," he said, his eyes focused on the wall across from them. "It's risky, but it might be our best shot at getting the information we need."

Jazz looked up at him, her curiosity piqued. "What is it?"

Dev hesitated for a moment before continuing. "We've been playing defense this whole time, trying to react to what they throw at us. But what if we changed the game? What if we went on the offensive?"

Jazz raised an eyebrow, intrigued by the idea. "How do you mean?"

"I've been thinking about setting a trap," Dev explained, his mind already working out the details. "We could create a fake vulnerability, something that looks like a weak spot in our defenses. If we make it convincing enough, they might take the bait. And when they do, we'll be ready."

Jazz considered the plan, weighing the risks and rewards. It was dangerous, no doubt about it, but it was also the kind of bold move that could give them the upper hand. And right now, they needed every advantage they could get.

"It's risky," she said finally, her voice steady. "But it could work. If we're careful."

Dev nodded, his expression serious. "We'll have to be. One wrong move, and it could backfire. But if we pull it off, we might finally get the evidence we need to take them down."

Jazz took a deep breath, her resolve hardening. "Let's do it, then. I'm tired of playing defense. It's time we took the fight to them."

Dev smiled, a sense of renewed purpose filling him. "Alright. Let's do this."

Over the next few days, they threw themselves into the task of setting up the trap. Dev worked tirelessly, creating a convincing fake vulnerability in their systems, one that was designed to lure their enemies in. He made sure every detail was perfect, knowing that they couldn't afford any mistakes.

Jazz, meanwhile, used her connections to spread the word, planting the seeds that would lead their enemies to the trap. It was a delicate balance—one wrong move, and the whole plan could come crashing down. But together, they worked seamlessly, their combined skills creating a web of deception that would be hard to resist.

As the day of the trap approached, the tension between them shifted from frustration to anticipation. They knew the risks, but they also knew that this was their best chance at turning the tables. They were playing with fire, but it was a fire they were willing to risk getting burned by if it meant achieving their goal.

The night before the trap was set to go off, they sat together in the dimly lit living room, the weight of what they were about to do hanging in the air between them. There was no need for words; they both knew what was at stake. Instead, they found comfort in the silence, in the presence of each other, as they prepared for the battle ahead.

As they sat there, Jazz reached out and took Dev's hand, her fingers intertwining with his. "No matter what happens tomorrow," she said softly, her voice filled with determination, "I want you to know that I'm glad we're doing this together. I wouldn't want to face this with anyone else."

Dev squeezed her hand, his heart swelling with emotion. "I feel the same way, Jazz. We're stronger together. And tomorrow, we're going to prove that."

The next day dawned with a sense of purpose. They were ready, their plan meticulously laid out, their resolve unshakable. They had faced so many challenges already, but this was the moment that would define their fight.

As the day unfolded, they watched and waited, every nerve on edge as they monitored the trap. The hours seemed to stretch on endlessly, each minute feeling like an eternity. But then, finally, they saw the signs they had been waiting for—someone had taken the bait.

Dev's heart raced as he watched the data stream across the screen, the signs of the intrusion clear as day. "They're in," he said, his voice tense with anticipation. "This is it, Jazz. This is our chance."

Jazz leaned in closer, her eyes locked on the screen. "Let's see who we're dealing with."

As they traced the intruder's movements, following the digital trail back to its source, the pieces of the puzzle began to fall into place. The identity of their enemy was revealed, and with it, a shocking truth that neither of them had expected.

But just as they were about to seize their victory, something went wrong. The screen flickered, the data streams shifting in a way that shouldn't have been possible. Dev's heart dropped as he realized what was happening.

"They're countering us," he said, his voice filled with disbelief. "They knew we were setting a trap. They were waiting for us."

Panic surged through Jazz as she watched the screen, the realization of their situation hitting her like a ton of bricks. "What do we do, Dev? How do we stop this?"

Dev's mind raced as he tried to think of a way to regain control, but the situation was spiraling out of their hands. The intruder's counterattack was relentless, tearing through their defenses with a precision that was terrifyingly effective.

"We need to shut it down," Dev said, his fingers flying over the keyboard as he tried to close the backdoor they had created. "If we don't stop them now, they'll get everything. We'll lose everything."

Jazz watched in horror as the situation unfolded, her heart pounding in her chest. They had been so close—so close to winning, to finally putting an end to the nightmare. But now, it was all falling apart, and she didn't know how to stop it.

As Dev worked furiously to regain control, the intruder's attack intensified, the screen flashing with warnings and errors. It was a race against time, and they were losing.

But just as all hope seemed lost, a miracle happened. Dev's fingers found the right sequence, the right combination of commands, and the screen suddenly went dark. The attack had been stopped; the backdoor closed just in time.

They had survived. But the cost of their survival was a chilling realization—they were facing an enemy more powerful and more cunning than they had ever imagined. And as they sat there, the adrenaline still coursing through their veins, they both knew that this was just the beginning of a much larger battle.

Chapter 8: Encrypted Emotions

The silence in the room was deafening as the screen in front of Devon and Jazz went dark. The flickering lights of the city outside their window seemed distant, almost irrelevant in the wake of what had just happened. They had come face-to-face with a powerful adversary, one who had anticipated their every move, and the realization left a cold knot of fear in the pit of their stomachs.

Dev leaned back in his chair, his hands trembling slightly as the adrenaline began to fade. He had always prided himself on being calm under pressure, but this time, the stakes were higher than ever before. They had narrowly escaped disaster, but the victory felt hollow, overshadowed by the knowledge that their enemy was still out there, watching, waiting for their next move.

Jazz sat beside him, her face pale, her eyes wide with a mix of fear and disbelief. "We almost lost everything," she whispered, her voice barely audible. "They were ready for us, Dev. They knew exactly what we were doing."

Dev nodded, his mind racing as he tried to process everything that had just happened. "They're smarter than we thought," he said, his voice laced with frustration. "We underestimated them, and it nearly cost us."

Jazz's hands were clenched into fists in her lap, her knuckles white. "What do we do now? How do we fight back against someone who's always one step ahead?"

Dev didn't have an immediate answer. For the first time in a long while, he felt genuinely outmatched. But he knew that giving up wasn't an option. He had promised to protect Jazz, to see this through to the end, and he wasn't about to break that promise now.

"We regroup," Dev said finally, his voice firm despite the doubt that gnawed at him. "We need to rethink our strategy. They know our moves, so we have to do something they won't expect. We need to be unpredictable, to turn their advantage against them."

Jazz looked at him, searching his eyes for any sign of hesitation. She found none. Despite everything, Dev was determined to keep fighting, to find a way to win. It was one of the things she admired most about him—his unwavering resolve, even in the face of overwhelming odds.

"I trust you, Dev," she said softly, her voice filled with a mix of gratitude and determination. "I know we can do this. We just have to stay one step ahead."

Dev smiled faintly, the warmth of her words cutting through the cold fear that had gripped him. "We will, Jazz. We've come too far to give up now."

But as the hours passed, and they continued to work late into the night, the weight of their situation began to take its toll. They were both exhausted, mentally and physically, and the constant pressure was starting to wear them down. The trust they had built between them was strong, but the strain of their mission was beginning to show.

One evening, after another long day of trying to outmaneuver their enemies, Jazz found herself alone in the living room, staring out the window at the city below. The weight of everything they had been through pressed down on her like a heavy blanket, suffocating and relentless. She had always been strong, always prided herself on her ability to handle anything life threw at her. But now, she felt like she was unraveling, bit by bit.

She didn't hear Dev approach until he was standing right beside her, his presence a comforting warmth in the otherwise cold room. "Penny for your thoughts?" he asked, his voice gentle.

Jazz sighed, leaning her head against the cool glass of the window. "I don't know, Dev. I'm just... tired. Tired of fighting, of being scared all the time. I want this to be over, but I don't know how much more I can take."

Dev reached out, placing a reassuring hand on her shoulder. "I know it's hard, Jazz. But we're in this together. You're not alone."

Jazz turned to look at him, her eyes glistening with unshed tears. "I know that, and I'm grateful. But I'm scared, Dev. Scared of losing you, of losing everything we've fought for. I've never felt this way before, and it's terrifying."

Dev's heart ached at her words. He could see the fear in her eyes, the vulnerability she rarely let anyone see. He reached up, gently brushing a stray tear from her cheek. "I'm scared too," he admitted, his voice filled with a raw honesty that surprised even him. "But I'm not going anywhere, Jazz. We're going to get through this, and when we do, we'll finally have the life we deserve."

Jazz looked into his eyes, searching for the strength she needed. And in that moment, she found it—not just in him, but in the bond, they shared, the love that had grown between them despite the odds. It was a love that had been forged in the fires of danger and fear, but it was also a love that had the power to overcome anything.

Without thinking, she reached up and pulled him into a kiss, pouring all of her fear, her frustration, and her love into that one act. Dev responded immediately, his arms wrapping around her as he kissed her back with a passion that took her breath away. For a moment, the world outside their window ceased to exist, and all that mattered was the connection between them, the fire that burned so brightly in their hearts.

When they finally pulled apart, both of them were breathing heavily, their foreheads resting against each other as they tried to catch their breath. "I love you, Dev," Jazz whispered, her voice filled with emotion. "I don't know what I would do without you."

Dev smiled, his heart swelling with love for the woman in his arms. "I love you too, Jazz. And you're never going to have to find out. We're in this together, now and always."

They stood there for a long time, wrapped in each other's arms, finding comfort in the love they shared. The road ahead was still uncertain, and the dangers they faced were more real than ever. But in that moment, they knew that as long as they had each other, they could face anything.

The next morning, they woke up with a renewed sense of purpose. The fear that had hung over them like a cloud was still there, but it was tempered by the love and trust they had for each other. They were stronger together, and they knew that no matter what happened, they would face it as a team.

As they sat down at the table to plan their next move, Dev looked over at Jazz, his eyes filled with determination. "We're going to win this, Jazz," he said, his voice steady. "We're going to take them down, and we're going to get our lives back."

Jazz nodded, her resolve firm. "I know we will. But we have to be smart, Dev. We can't afford any more mistakes."

Dev agreed, his mind already working on their next strategy. "We need to find out who's behind this, who's pulling the strings. If we can expose them, we can cut off their power at the source."

Jazz leaned forward, her eyes narrowing as she thought. "There's one person who might have the answers we need. Someone who's been in the shadows, but who might be willing to help us if we can convince them, it's in their best interest."

Dev raised an eyebrow, intrigued. "Who?"

Jazz hesitated for a moment before speaking. "There's a hacker I used to work with, someone who knows the ins and outs of the underground tech world better than anyone. They've always been a bit of a wild card, but if anyone can help us, it's them."

Dev considered her words, weighing the risks and benefits. It was a long shot, but at this point, they needed every advantage they could get. "Do you think they'll talk to us?"

Jazz shrugged. "There's only one way to find out. But if we approach them the right way, if we offer them something they want, they might be willing to help."

Dev nodded, his mind already racing with possibilities. "Alright. Let's set up a meeting. But we need to be careful. If this person is as good as you say they are, they'll know we're coming."

Jazz smiled, a hint of her old confidence returning. "Leave that to me. I know how to handle them."

As they prepared to reach out to the mysterious hacker, both of them knew that this could be the turning point in their fight. The risks were high, but the potential rewards were even higher. They were playing a dangerous game, but it was a game they were determined to win.

The following days were filled with careful planning and preparation. Jazz made contact with the hacker, using her old connections to arrange a discreet meeting. It wasn't easy—this person was notoriously elusive and convincing them to help would be no small feat. But Jazz was persistent, and after several days of back-and-forth communication, they finally secured a meeting.

The location was a small, out-of-the-way café in a quiet part of the city. It was the kind of place where people went to be forgotten, where anonymity was the currency of choice. As they arrived, Jazz and Dev both felt the weight of what they were about to do. This meeting could change everything, for better or worse.

They entered the café and found a table in the back, away from prying eyes. They didn't have to wait long before the hacker arrived—a tall, slender figure dressed in a dark hoodie and jeans, their face obscured by a pair of large sunglasses and a baseball cap. They moved with a quiet confidence, their every step calculated and deliberate.

The hacker approached their table and sat down without a word; their posture relaxed but alert. Jazz and Dev exchanged a brief glance before Jazz spoke.

Chapter 9: The Network of Trust

They moved with a quiet confidence, their every step measured and deliberate. As the hacker approached the table, Jazz and Devon exchanged a quick glance, their unspoken understanding clear—they needed this person on their side, and they couldn't afford any missteps.

The hacker slid into the seat opposite them, their posture relaxed but alert. Even through the sunglasses and cap, it was clear they were assessing the situation, reading every detail, every nuance. For a moment, no one spoke, the tension hanging in the air like a thick fog.

Finally, Jazz broke the silence, her voice calm and controlled. "Thanks for meeting with us. We appreciate your time."

The hacker leaned back slightly, crossing their arms over their chest. "I don't do this often," they said, their voice low and smooth, betraying no emotion. "So, make it worth my while. Why should I help you?"

Devon watched Jazz closely, knowing this was her moment. She had a history with this person, a relationship built on mutual respect and shared experiences. If anyone could convince them to join their cause, it was her.

"We're in a bad spot," Jazz began, her tone direct. "And I think you know that. You've always been good at reading the currents, knowing when to swim with the tide and when to go against it. Right now, we're up against something bigger than we've ever faced, and we need someone with your skills to help level the playing field."

The hacker didn't respond immediately, their expression hidden behind the sunglasses. They were clearly weighing their options, considering Jazz's words carefully.

"Big talk," the hacker finally said, their tone neutral. "But you know as well as I do that talk is cheap. What's in it for me?"

Jazz nodded, as if expecting the question. "We're not just asking for a favor. We know you have your own interests, your own agenda. We can help each other. We're sitting on some valuable information—things that could be useful to you, if you're willing to work with us."

Devon watched as the hacker's posture shifted slightly, a subtle sign that they were intrigued. He knew Jazz was playing a delicate game, offering just enough to spark interest without revealing too much. It was a dangerous dance, but one she was skilled at.

The hacker tapped their fingers on the table, considering the offer. "You've got my attention," they said slowly. "But I need more than just promises. I need to know that you're serious."

Jazz didn't hesitate. "We are. We're willing to share what we know, but we need your help to dig deeper. This isn't just about surviving—it's about turning the tables, taking control of the situation. And I think you'll agree, that's something worth fighting for."

The hacker was silent for a long moment, the only sound in the café the distant hum of conversation and the clinking of dishes. Devon could feel the tension in the air, the weight of the decision hanging over them. If they couldn't convince this person to join their cause, they would lose a crucial ally—and with it, their best chance of taking down the enemies closing in on them.

Finally, the hacker leaned forward, lowering their voice to a whisper. "You've always had guts, Jazz. I'll give you that. And I like the idea of flipping the script on these bastards. But this won't be easy. If we do this, we're all in—no turning back. You sure you're ready for that?"

Jazz didn't hesitate. "We're ready. Whatever it takes."

The hacker studied her for a moment longer, then nodded. "Alright. I'm in. But if we're going to do this, we do it my way. No half-measures. No second-guessing."

Jazz nodded in agreement. "Deal. We're putting our trust in you."

The hacker reached up, pulling off their sunglasses and revealing sharp, calculating eyes that seemed to see right through them. "Good. Because trust is the only currency that matters in this game. And if you break that trust, you'll lose more than just this fight."

Devon felt a chill run down his spine at the hacker's words. This person was dangerous, no doubt about it. But they were also exactly what they needed—someone who could navigate the dark, tangled web of their enemies' operations with ease, someone who understood the stakes and wasn't afraid to take risks.

With the deal made, they spent the next hour going over the details, laying the groundwork for their new alliance. The hacker, who went by the alias "Cipher," proved to be as sharp and resourceful as Jazz had promised. They had a deep network of contacts, access to resources Devon could only dream of, and a strategic mind that rivaled his own.

As they discussed their plan, Cipher outlined a series of moves designed to undermine their enemies' operations, exploiting weaknesses and turning their own tactics against them. It was a bold strategy, one that would require careful execution and perfect timing. But if it worked, it could shift the balance of power in their favor.

"We start by creating a series of diversions," Cipher explained, their voice low and measured. "We'll hit them from multiple angles, force them to spread their resources thin. While they're scrambling to contain the damage, we'll target their communication networks. Cut off their lines of command, and they'll be vulnerable."

Devon nodded, impressed by the thoroughness of the plan. It was exactly the kind of strategy they needed—aggressive, calculated, and designed to exploit their enemies' arrogance.

"But we have to be careful," Cipher continued, their gaze flicking between Devon and Jazz. "One wrong move, and they'll know we're onto them. We have to make every action count, keep them guessing until it's too late."

Jazz leaned forward; her expression focused. "And what about the leadership? We need to identify who's pulling the strings, who's behind all of this."

Cipher smiled faintly, a hint of amusement in their eyes. "Don't worry. I've got some ideas on how to flush them out. But that's the final move. First, we weaken their infrastructure, destabilize their operations. Once they're off balance, we make our move on the leadership."

The plan was ambitious, but it was exactly what they needed—a way to take control of the situation, to go on the offensive rather than constantly reacting to their enemies' moves. Devon could feel a sense of hope returning, a renewed belief that they could win this fight.

As the meeting wrapped up, Cipher stood, slipping their sunglasses back on and pulling their cap low over their eyes. "I'll be in touch," they said, their voice cool and confident. "But remember—this only works if we trust each other. No secrets, no second-guessing. We're in this together now."

Jazz nodded, her expression serious. "Understood. We won't let you down."

With a final nod, Cipher turned and left the café, disappearing into the crowd outside. As the door closed behind them, Devon let out a breath he hadn't realized he was holding. The meeting had gone better than he had hoped, but the weight of what lay ahead still pressed down on him.

Jazz reached across the table, taking his hand in hers. "We can do this, Dev," she said, her voice filled with quiet determination. "We're not alone anymore. We have a chance."

Devon squeezed her hand, his resolve strengthening. "Yeah, we do. And we're going to make it count."

Over the next few days, they threw themselves into the work, following Cipher's plan with precision and care. They created diversions, launched cyber-attacks, and sowed confusion among their enemies. It was a delicate operation, one that required constant vigilance and quick thinking. But with Cipher's guidance, they began to see results.

Their enemies were on the defensive, their operations disrupted, and their communication lines compromised. It was a small victory, but it gave them the momentum they needed. And as they continued to push forward, Devon and Jazz found themselves growing closer, their bond strengthened by the challenges they faced together.

But even as they made progress, the danger remained ever-present. They were playing a high-stakes game, and one wrong move could spell disaster. The fear was always there, lurking in the back of their minds, a constant reminder of the risks they were taking.

One night, after a particularly tense day, Devon and Jazz sat together on the couch, the weight of their mission heavy on their shoulders. The apartment was quiet, the only sound the distant hum of the city outside. They were both exhausted, but sleep was elusive, their minds too full of what lay ahead.

Jazz leaned her head against Devon's shoulder, her eyes closed as she tried to find a moment of peace. "Do you ever wonder what our lives would be like if we weren't caught up in all of this?" she asked softly.

Devon wrapped his arm around her, pulling her closer. "Yeah, I do. Sometimes I think about what it would be like to just... walk away. To leave all of this behind and start fresh somewhere else."

Jazz smiled faintly, the thought both comforting and bittersweet. "It's a nice dream. But I don't think we're the kind of people who can just walk away."

Devon nodded, knowing she was right. They were both too deeply entrenched in this fight, too committed to seeing it through to the end. But that didn't stop him from wishing, just for a moment, that things could be different.

"Once this is over," he said quietly, "we'll find a way to have a normal life. We'll leave this behind and build something new. Together."

Jazz looked up at him, her eyes filled with a mixture of hope and uncertainty. "You really think that's possible?"

Devon met her gaze, his expression serious. "I do. We just have to get through this first."

Jazz nodded, her hand reaching up to touch his cheek. "I want that, Dev. More than anything."

They sat in silence for a while, finding comfort in each other's presence. The road ahead was still long, and the dangers they faced were far from over. But they had each other, and that was enough to keep them going.

As the night wore on, they finally allowed themselves to drift off to sleep, holding each other close. The world outside might be filled with uncertainty and danger, but in that moment, they found peace in the simple act of being together.

And as they slept, the wheels of their plan continued to turn, setting the stage for the final act of their fight. The network of trust they had built with Cipher was strong, but it would be tested in the days to come. The game was far from over, and their enemies were not about to go down without a fight.

But Devon and Jazz were ready. They had come too far, faced too much, to back down now. They were in this together, and they would see it through to the end—no matter what it took.

Chapter 10: Hacked by Love

The days following their meeting with Cipher were a whirlwind of activity. Devon and Jazz found themselves entrenched in the complex web of their enemies' operations; their every move carefully calculated to push their adversaries further into disarray. The strategy was working—slowly but surely, they were chipping away at the foundation of their opponents' power. But with every victory came a deeper understanding of the forces they were up against.

As they delved deeper into the network of corruption and deceit, Devon and Jazz uncovered a tangled web of alliances, betrayals, and hidden agendas. The deeper they went, the more they realized just how far-reaching their enemies' influence was. It wasn't just about them anymore—this fight had the potential to affect countless lives, to expose secrets that powerful people would kill to keep hidden.

But even as the stakes grew higher, Devon and Jazz found themselves drawing closer together. The constant danger, the shared struggle—it all served to strengthen the bond between them. They had started this journey as two individuals with their own goals, their own fears. But now, they were a team, their fates intertwined in a way that neither of them had anticipated.

One evening, as they sat in the dim light of Devon's apartment, going over the latest data Cipher had provided, Jazz couldn't help but feel a sense of awe at how far they had come. It hadn't been long ago that they were strangers, brought together by circumstance and a shared goal. Now, they were partners in every sense of the word—working together, fighting together, and falling deeper in love with each passing day.

Devon looked up from the screen, catching her staring at him. "What's on your mind?" he asked, a small smile playing at the corners of his lips.

Jazz hesitated for a moment, then shrugged, her expression softening. "Just thinking about how much things have changed. How much we've changed."

Devon leaned back in his chair, his gaze thoughtful. "Yeah, it's been a hell of a ride, hasn't it? I didn't expect any of this when we first met."

"Neither did I," Jazz admitted. "But I'm glad it happened. I'm glad we found each other."

Devon's smile widened, a warmth spreading through his chest. "Me too, Jazz. I can't imagine going through this with anyone else."

They shared a quiet moment, the weight of their journey settling over them like a blanket. The road ahead was still fraught with danger, but they had each other—and that was a source of strength that no enemy could take away.

As they turned their attention back to the task at hand, Cipher's latest data revealed something that sent a chill down Devon's spine. It was a pattern—a series of communications that seemed innocuous at first glance, but upon closer inspection, revealed a network of covert operations stretching across multiple countries. The implications were staggering.

"Jazz, look at this," Devon said, his voice low and urgent. "This isn't just a local operation. It's global. They've got connections everywhere—finance, politics, military. This is bigger than we thought."

Jazz leaned in, her eyes scanning the data. The gravity of what they were uncovering hit her like a punch to the gut. "These changes everything," she murmured. "If we're going to take them down, we need to expose all of it. But that's going to make us even bigger targets."

Devon nodded, his mind racing. "We'll need to be careful. We can't just go public with this—we need to gather more evidence, make sure we've got an airtight case. And we need to figure out who's at the top, who's orchestrating all of this."

Jazz's heart pounded in her chest as she considered the enormity of the task ahead. But even as the fear threatened to creep in, she felt a steely resolve settle over her. This was why they had started this fight—to uncover the truth, to bring justice to those who had been wronged. And now that they were on the verge of something big, she wasn't about to back down.

"We're going to need help," Jazz said, her voice firm. "Cipher's good, but we'll need more allies if we're going to take this all the way. People we can trust."

Devon nodded in agreement. "I know a few people who might be able to help—old contacts, people who've been in the game for a long time. But we'll need to approach them carefully. We can't let anyone know what we're planning until we're ready to move."

As they began to formulate a plan, the tension between them grew, not out of fear, but out of the magnitude of what they were about to undertake. This wasn't just about survival anymore—it was about bringing down a global network of corruption and power, and the risks were higher than ever.

But despite the danger, despite the uncertainty, Devon and Jazz found solace in each other. The nights they spent together, holding each other close as the world outside seemed to close in, became a sanctuary—a place where they could forget, if only for a little while, the weight of the mission they had undertaken.

One night, after a particularly long day of planning and strategizing, Jazz found herself unable to sleep. She lay awake in bed, the events of the past few weeks swirling in her mind. The fear, the adrenaline, the constant pressure—it was all beginning to take its toll.

But even as the doubts threatened to overwhelm her, she felt Devon's arm around her, pulling her close.

"You, okay?" he murmured, his voice thick with sleep.

Jazz sighed, her heart aching with a mixture of love and anxiety. "I'm just thinking about everything. How far we've come, and how much further we have to go."

Devon tightened his hold on her, his warmth seeping into her bones. "We're going to get through this, Jazz. I know it's hard, but we've got each other. And that's more than enough."

Jazz turned to face him, her hand reaching up to caress his cheek. "I don't know what I'd do without you, Dev. You've been my rock through all of this."

Devon smiled, leaning in to kiss her gently. "We're in this together, remember? You're not alone."

They lay there in the dark, their hearts beating in sync as they held each other close. The world outside might be filled with danger and uncertainty, but in that moment, they found peace in the love they shared—a love that had grown stronger with each passing day, forged in the fires of adversity.

As the days turned into weeks, their plan began to take shape. With Cipher's help, they identified key players in the network, gathering the evidence they needed to expose the entire operation. It was painstaking work, but with each new piece of information, they came closer to their goal.

But as they prepared to make their move, the stakes grew higher. Their enemies were becoming more desperate, more dangerous. Devon and Jazz knew that they were running out of time—the closer they got to the truth, the more likely it was that their enemies would strike back.

One evening, as they sat together in their apartment, Devon received a message from one of his contacts—an old friend who had connections in high places. The message was brief, but it sent a chill down his spine.

They know you're coming. Be careful.

Devon stared at the screen, his heart pounding. This was it—their enemies were on to them, and the window for action was closing fast.

"We have to move now," Devon said, his voice urgent. "They know we're coming. If we don't act soon, they'll shut us down before we can expose them."

Jazz nodded, her expression serious. "Then we go all in. We hit them hard and fast, before they have a chance to react."

They spent the next few hours finalizing their plan, knowing that this was their last chance to take down the network. It was a dangerous gamble, but they had come too far to turn back now.

As the night wore on, they found themselves sitting together on the couch, the weight of the impending showdown pressing down on them. There was so much they wanted to say, so much that had been left unsaid. But in that moment, words seemed inadequate.

Instead, they simply held each other, finding comfort in the warmth of their embrace. The fear, the anxiety, the uncertainty—it all melted away in the face of the love they shared, a love that had grown stronger with each challenge they faced.

"I love you, Jazz," Devon whispered, his voice filled with emotion. "No matter what happens, I want you to know that."

Jazz looked up at him, her eyes glistening with unshed tears. "I love you too, Dev. More than I ever thought possible."

They kissed, a slow, lingering kiss that spoke of all the things they couldn't put into words. In that moment, nothing else mattered—only the two of them, together, facing whatever came their way.

When they finally pulled apart, Jazz rested her head on Devon's chest, listening to the steady beat of his heart. "We're going to make it through this," she whispered, as much to herself as to him. "We have to."

Devon tightened his hold on her, his resolve firm. "We will. We're in this together, and we're not backing down."

As the first light of dawn began to creep through the window, they knew it was time to act. The final phase of their plan was about to begin, and there was no turning back.

They got dressed in silence, their movements quick and efficient as they prepared for what lay ahead. Devon checked his gear, making sure everything was in place, while Jazz went over the plan one last time, her mind focused on the task at hand.

When they were ready, they shared one last look, a silent acknowledgment of everything they had been through, and everything that was still to come. Then, without another word, they left the apartment, stepping out into the early morning light.

The city was quiet, the streets empty as they made their way to the rendezvous point. They were met by Cipher, who had been working behind the scenes to ensure everything was in place. The hacker was calm, composed, but Devon could sense the tension beneath the surface. This was it—the moment they had all been working toward.

"Are you ready?" Cipher asked, their voice steady.

Devon and Jazz nodded, their resolve unshakable. "We're ready," Jazz said, her voice filled with determination.

Cipher gave a curt nod, then handed them each a small device—a compact piece of tech designed to infiltrate and disrupt the network's communications. It was the key to their plan, the tool that would bring down the entire operation.

"You know what to do," Cipher said, their gaze intense. "Once you're inside, there's no turning back. Make every move count."

Devon and Jazz exchanged one last look, then turned and headed toward the building that housed the heart of their enemies' operations. The plan was simple in theory, but in practice, it was a high-stakes gamble that could go wrong at any moment.

They approached the building with caution, using every bit of skill and knowledge they had gained over the years to avoid detection. The tension was palpable, the adrenaline pumping through their veins as they navigated the maze of security measures and surveillance systems.

When they finally reached their target, Devon and Jazz moved quickly, setting the devices in place and activating the program that would bring down the network. The screens in front of them flickered to life, displaying lines of code as the system began to unravel.

But just as they were about to complete the final step, the alarms blared. They had been discovered.

Devon's heart raced as he realized what was happening. They had been too late—their enemies had anticipated their move, and now the building was on lockdown.

"We have to get out of here," Devon said urgently, grabbing Jazz's hand as they prepared to make their escape.

But before they could move, the door burst open, and a group of armed men stormed in, their weapons trained on Devon and Jazz. They were surrounded.

Devon's mind raced, his thoughts a blur as he tried to find a way out. But the situation was dire, and he knew they were out of options.

Jazz looked at him, her eyes filled with fear but also a steely resolve. "Dev, no matter what happens, I want you to know that I love you. I'm not afraid."

Devon's heart ached as he looked at the woman he loved, knowing that this might be the end. "I love you too, Jazz. We're going to get through this. We have to."

But even as he said the words, he knew that the odds were against them. They had come so far, fought so hard, but now they were cornered, with no way out.

The leader of the armed men stepped forward, a cold smile on his face as he looked at Devon and Jazz. "You thought you could take us down?" he sneered. "You have no idea who you're dealing with."

Devon's grip tightened on Jazz's hand, his mind racing for a solution. But before he could act, the man raised his weapon, his finger on the trigger.

In that moment, time seemed to slow down. Devon's thoughts were a whirlwind of fear and regret, but also love—a love so powerful that it eclipsed everything else.

And then, just as the man was about to pull the trigger, the lights in the room flickered, and the screens on the walls erupted in a cascade of static. Devon's heart skipped a beat as he realized what was happening—Cipher had activated the final phase of their plan, a last-ditch effort to disrupt the network's systems.

The armed men hesitated; their attention momentarily diverted by the chaos unfolding on the screens. It was the opening Devon and Jazz needed.

Without a second thought, Devon lunged at the leader, knocking him off balance as Jazz grabbed one of the fallen weapons. The room erupted in a flurry of motion as Devon and Jazz fought back with everything they had, using their training and instincts to overpower their attackers.

It was a brutal, desperate fight, but they were fueled by adrenaline and determination. They had come too far to lose now.

As the last of their attackers fell, Devon and Jazz stood in the middle of the room, their breathing heavy, their bodies bruised but still standing. The alarms were still blaring, but they had no time to think about the chaos around them.

"Dev, we need to go, now!" Jazz urged, her voice urgent.

Devon nodded, his mind still reeling from the events of the past few minutes. They had survived, but they were far from safe.

They sprinted toward the exit, their hearts pounding as they navigated the maze of hallways and security measures. The building was in chaos, the network's systems on the brink of collapse.

When they finally burst through the doors and into the cool night air, Devon felt a wave of relief wash over him. They had made it—barely, but they had made it.

But even as they caught their breath, Devon knew that this was far from over. They had dealt a blow to their enemies, but the fight was still ahead of them.

As they made their way to the rendezvous point where Cipher was waiting, Devon reached out and took Jazz's hand, his grip firm and reassuring.

"We did it, Jazz," he said, his voice filled with a mix of exhaustion and determination. "We're still standing."

Jazz looked at him, a small smile playing on her lips despite the tension in her eyes. "Yeah, we did. But we've got a lot more to do."

Devon nodded, knowing she was right. They had won a battle, but the war was still ahead of them.

When they reached the rendezvous point, Cipher was waiting, their expression unreadable. "You pulled it off," they said, a note of respect in their voice. "I wasn't sure you would."

Devon and Jazz exchanged a look, their exhaustion evident. "We're not done yet," Jazz said, her voice steady. "There's still more to do. But we're ready."

Cipher nodded, their gaze thoughtful. "Good. Because this fight isn't over. But with what you've just done, we've got a real chance. Let's finish this."

And with that, they turned and headed into the night, ready to face whatever came next. The road ahead was still uncertain, but they knew that as long as they had each other, they could face anything.

Together, they were unstoppable.

Chapter 11: The Algorithm of Attraction

The night air was crisp as Devon, Jazz, and Cipher disappeared into the labyrinth of city streets. The adrenaline that had fueled their narrow escape was fading, replaced by the cold, hard reality of what lay ahead. They had struck a blow, but their enemies were still out there, regrouping, planning their next move. Devon could feel the weight of the task ahead pressing down on him, but he refused to let it break him. He wasn't just fighting for survival anymore—he was fighting for the life he wanted with Jazz.

As they walked in silence, their footsteps echoing in the deserted streets, Devon couldn't help but steal glances at Jazz. She was a picture of quiet determination, her face set in a mask of resolve. But he knew her well enough by now to see the exhaustion beneath the surface, the fear she was trying so hard to hide. He wanted to reach out to her, to tell her that everything would be okay, but he knew that words alone wouldn't be enough. They had to keep moving forward, one step at a time.

Cipher led them to a safe house—a nondescript building tucked away in a forgotten corner of the city. It was the kind of place that blended into the background, where no one would think to look for them. Inside, the walls were bare, the furniture sparse, but it was secure, and that was all that mattered.

As soon as they were inside, Cipher began setting up their equipment, their movements precise and efficient. Devon and Jazz exchanged a glance, then silently agreed to give Cipher the space they needed to work. They retreated to a small room at the back of the house, where they could catch their breath and plan their next move.

The room was dark, the only light coming from a single lamp in the corner. Devon sat down on the edge of the bed, running a hand through his hair as he tried to gather his thoughts. Jazz remained standing; her arms crossed over her chest as she stared out the window at the empty street below.

"Are you okay?" Devon asked softly, breaking the silence.

Jazz didn't turn around, her gaze still fixed on the window. "I don't know," she admitted, her voice tinged with exhaustion. "I feel like we're constantly running, constantly looking over our shoulders. I'm tired, Dev. I'm tired of being afraid."

Devon stood and walked over to her, gently placing a hand on her shoulder. "I know," he said, his voice filled with understanding. "But we're almost there. We're so close to bringing this all down. Once it's over, we can finally stop running. We can finally have a life together."

Jazz turned to face him, her eyes searching his. "Do you really believe that? Do you really think we can just... walk away from all of this?"

Devon hesitated for a moment, then nodded. "Yes, I do. We've been through hell, Jazz, but we're still here. We're still fighting. And when this is over, I want to start a new life with you—a life where we don't have to look over our shoulders, where we can just be together."

Jazz's eyes softened, and she reached up to cup his face in her hands. "I want that too," she whispered. "More than anything."

They stood there for a long moment, the world outside fading away as they held each other close. In that small room, in the midst of the chaos that had become their lives, they found a moment of peace—a moment where the only thing that mattered was the love they shared.

But the peace was fleeting, and reality soon intruded. Cipher appeared in the doorway, their expression unreadable. "We've got a problem," they said, their tone brisk.

Devon and Jazz immediately pulled apart, their attention snapping back to the present. "What is it?" Devon asked, his heart sinking at the look on Cipher's face.

Cipher stepped into the room, holding up a tablet displaying a stream of data. "The network's been compromised. They know about the safe house. We've got to move, now."

Jazz's heart leaped into her throat. "How did they find us so quickly?"

Cipher's expression was grim. "I don't know, but we don't have time to figure it out. We need to get out of here before they close in."

Devon cursed under his breath, his mind racing. They had just barely escaped with their lives, and now they were on the run again. The thought of losing Jazz, of failing after they had come so far, was unbearable. But there was no time for hesitation.

"We'll split up," Devon said, his voice decisive. "It'll be harder for them to track us that way. We'll meet up at the secondary safe house."

Cipher nodded in agreement. "I'll wipe the systems here. They won't be able to trace anything back to us."

Jazz's heart pounded as she grabbed her jacket, her mind spinning with fear and uncertainty. But as she looked at Devon, she felt a surge of determination. They had come too far to give up now.

"Be careful," Devon said, his voice low as he pulled her into a quick, fierce embrace. "We'll get through this, Jazz. I promise."

Jazz nodded, squeezing his hand one last time before they separated. She could feel the weight of his promise in her heart, and it gave her the strength she needed to keep going.

They left the safe house in silence, each of them heading in a different direction. The streets were eerily quiet, the city bathed in the soft glow of streetlights. Jazz moved quickly, keeping to the shadows as she navigated the maze of alleyways and backstreets. Her mind was a blur of thoughts, her senses on high alert for any sign of danger.

As she made her way through the city, she couldn't help but think about everything that had brought her to this moment. The years of running, the battles she had fought, the people she had lost—it had all led her here, to this fight for her life and the life she wanted with Devon. And now, as they faced their greatest challenge yet, she knew that she couldn't afford to fail.

But just as she rounded a corner, her instincts screamed at her to stop. She froze, her breath catching in her throat as she spotted a figure lurking in the shadows up ahead. Her heart pounded in her chest as she quickly assessed the situation. There was no way to go back without being seen, and she couldn't risk a confrontation out in the open.

She pressed herself against the wall, her mind racing as she tried to come up with a plan. But before she could move, the figure stepped forward, revealing themselves in the dim light.

It was someone she recognized—one of the men who had attacked them earlier, his face twisted in a cruel smile as he spotted her.

"Going somewhere?" he sneered, his voice dripping with malice.

Jazz's blood ran cold. She was trapped, with no way out. But she refused to let fear paralyze her. She had come too far, fought too hard, to let it end like this.

Without hesitation, she reached for the small knife she kept hidden in her jacket, her hand steady as she prepared to defend herself. The man advanced, his eyes gleaming with sadistic pleasure as he closed the distance between them.

But just as he reached for her, a figure appeared out of the shadows, moving with lightning speed. There was a brief struggle, a flash of metal, and then the man crumpled to the ground, his eyes wide with shock as he bled out onto the pavement.

Jazz's heart raced as she stared at the man's lifeless body, her mind struggling to process what had just happened. But then she looked up and saw who had saved her.

It was Cipher, their expression calm and composed as they wiped the blood from the blade. "We need to keep moving," they said, their voice steady. "More will be coming."

Jazz nodded, her hands trembling as she tucked the knife back into her jacket. She knew Cipher was right—this was far from over.

They continued through the city, moving quickly and quietly as they made their way to the secondary safe house. The tension between them was palpable, but there was no time to dwell on what had just happened. They were in survival mode now, every step calculated, every move deliberates.

When they finally reached the safe house, Devon was already there, his face etched with worry. The relief in his eyes when he saw Jazz was palpable, and he pulled her into a tight embrace the moment she stepped through the door.

"I thought I'd lost you," he murmured, his voice thick with emotion.

"I'm here," Jazz whispered, holding him close. "I'm okay."

Cipher stood off to the side, their expression unreadable as they watched the reunion. "We don't have much time," they said, their tone brisk. "We need to move quickly if we're going to finish this."

Devon nodded; his arms still wrapped around Jazz. "What's the plan?"

Cipher pulled out their tablet, quickly accessing the data they had retrieved earlier. "We've pinpointed the location of the command center—the heart of their operation. If we can take it down, we'll cripple their entire network. But it's heavily guarded, and they'll be expecting us."

Jazz looked at the data, her mind racing. "How do we get in?"

Cipher's eyes narrowed as they studied the map. "There's a weakness in their defenses—a blind spot in their surveillance. If we time it right, we can slip in unnoticed. But we'll need to move fast, and we can't afford any mistakes."

Devon's jaw tightened as he looked at the map. "Then we make sure we don't make any. We take them down, once and for all."

The plan was set, and they moved quickly to prepare. There was no room for error, no time for hesitation. They were about to launch their final assault, and everything was on the line.

As they geared up, Jazz felt a sense of calm wash over her. This was it—the moment they had been fighting for, the moment that would determine their future. She glanced at Devon, who was checking his equipment with a focused intensity, and felt a surge of love and determination.

"We're going to do this," she said, her voice steady.

Devon looked up, his eyes meeting hers. "We are," he agreed. "And when it's over, we'll finally be free."

Cipher finished their preparations and nodded to Devon and Jazz. "Let's move."

They left the safe house under the cover of darkness, their movements silent and deliberate as they made their way to the command center. The city was eerily quiet, the tension thick in the air as they approached their target.

When they reached the blind spot in the surveillance, Cipher quickly disabled the remaining security measures, allowing them to slip through undetected. The command center loomed ahead, a fortress of steel and glass that housed the nerve center of their enemies' operation.

Jazz's heart pounded in her chest as they approached the entrance, her hand gripping her weapon tightly. This was it—the final showdown. They were about to bring down the people who had hunted them, who had tried to destroy them. And they were going to do it together.

As they entered the building, the air was charged with anticipation. The halls were empty, the silence oppressive as they moved deeper into the heart of the command center. Every step brought them closer to their goal, every heartbeat a reminder of the stakes.

When they finally reached the control room, Cipher quickly accessed the systems, disabling the remaining security protocols and initiating the shutdown sequence. The screens flickered, the data streams collapsing as the network began to implode.

But just as they were about to complete the final step, the door to the control room burst open, and a group of armed guards stormed in, their weapons trained on Devon, Jazz, and Cipher.

The room erupted into chaos as gunfire echoed through the halls. Devon and Jazz fought back with everything they had, their movements precise and deadly as they took down their attackers. Cipher worked frantically to finish the shutdown sequence, their fingers flying over the keyboard as the network continued to collapse.

But the fight was brutal, and they were outnumbered. Devon felt a sharp pain in his side as a bullet grazed him, but he pushed through the pain, his focus solely on protecting Jazz.

As the last of the guards fell, Cipher finally completed the sequence, and the screens in the control room went dark. The network was down, the operation crippled. They had done it.

But the victory was short-lived. The leader of the operation, a man they had only known by reputation, stepped into the room, his eyes cold and calculating as he surveyed the scene.

"You've made a grave mistake," he said, his voice dripping with venom. "You think you've won, but you've only delayed the inevitable."

Devon stepped forward; his weapon trained on the man. "It's over. You're finished."

The man's lips curled into a cruel smile. "You're naïve if you think this ends with me. There are others—powerful people who won't stop until you're dead. This is just the beginning."

Jazz felt a chill run down her spine at the man's words, but she refused to back down. "We'll take them all down, one by one. Just like we took you down."

The man's smile widened. "You're playing a dangerous game, girl. And in this game, there are no winners."

Before Devon or Jazz could react, the man pulled out a small device, a detonator, and pressed the button.

The room was suddenly filled with a blinding light, and Devon's world went dark.

Chapter 12: Dangerous Desires

The sound of an explosion echoed in Devon's ears as he slowly regained consciousness. His vision was blurred, and his body ached all over, but he could feel the cool, hard surface of the floor beneath him. Panic surged through him as he struggled to remember what had happened. The last thing he recalled was the leader pressing the detonator, and then everything went white.

Groaning in pain, Devon forced himself to sit up, his head spinning. The control room was in ruins, the walls scorched and the air thick with dust and smoke. Debris was scattered everywhere, and the acrid smell of burning electronics filled his nostrils. For a moment, all he could do was breathe, trying to piece together the fragments of his memory.

And then it hit him like a freight train: Jazz.

"Jazz!" Devon shouted, his voice hoarse as he scrambled to his feet, ignoring the pain that shot through his body. His heart pounded in his chest as he searched the room, his mind racing with fear. "Jazz, where are you?"

His eyes darted around the wreckage until he finally spotted her, lying a few feet away, motionless amidst the debris. The sight of her, so still and lifeless, sent a jolt of terror through him.

"No, no, no," Devon muttered as he stumbled over to her, his hands trembling as he knelt beside her. He reached out, gently brushing the dust and debris from her face, his heart in his throat. "Jazz, please, wake up. Please."

He placed his fingers on her neck, desperately searching for a pulse. For a moment, there was nothing, and Devon felt his world crumbling around him. But then he felt it—a faint, but steady beat beneath his fingertips.

A wave of relief crashed over him, and tears stung his eyes as he leaned over her, his voice trembling. "Thank God. Jazz, can you hear me? Come on, wake up. You're going to be okay."

Devon carefully cradled her head in his hands, his eyes scanning her body for any signs of serious injury. She was breathing, but it was shallow, and her face was pale, a thin line of blood trickling down her forehead from a small gash. The explosion had knocked her unconscious, but she was alive.

"Come on, Jazz," Devon whispered, his voice filled with urgency. "You need to wake up. We have to get out of here."

As if responding to his plea, Jazz's eyelids fluttered, and she let out a soft groan. Devon's heart leaped in his chest as he saw her slowly coming around. He gently stroked her cheek, his voice soft and reassuring. "That's it, Jazz. Come back to me."

Jazz's eyes slowly opened; her gaze unfocused as she tried to make sense of her surroundings. It took a moment for her to realize where she was, and when she finally did, her eyes widened in fear and confusion.

"Dev…" she croaked, her voice barely above a whisper. "What… what happened?"

Devon let out a shaky breath, relief flooding through him as he smiled down at her. "There was an explosion, but you're okay. We're okay."

Jazz blinked, trying to clear her head as she slowly pushed herself into a sitting position with Devon's help. Her body ached, and her head throbbed, but she was alive. She looked around at the ruined control room, her mind still trying to catch up with what had happened.

"Cipher… where's Cipher?" Jazz asked, her voice filled with concern.

Devon's expression darkened as he scanned the room again. In the chaos of the explosion, he hadn't noticed Cipher's absence. He looked around frantically, hoping to spot any sign of the hacker.

"Cipher!" Devon called out, his voice echoing in the wreckage. "Where are you?"

For a moment, there was no response, and Devon feared the worst. But then, from beneath a pile of debris on the far side of the room, he heard a faint groan.

Devon hurried over to the source of the sound, his heart pounding as he began to pull away the debris. He worked quickly, his hands moving with desperate speed as he uncovered Cipher's still form. The hacker was lying on their side, a piece of metal pinning them down, their face twisted in pain.

"Hang on, Cipher," Devon said urgently as he carefully lifted the metal off them. "We're going to get you out of here."

Cipher let out a pained breath as Devon helped them sit up, their eyes squeezed shut against the pain. "That... that bastard rigged the room," Cipher muttered, their voice strained. "We need to move... before reinforcements show up."

Devon nodded, his mind already racing with the urgency of the situation. He knew Cipher was right—they couldn't stay here. Their enemies would be closing in, and they were in no condition to fight.

Jazz, still groggy but determined, managed to get to her feet, wincing as she leaned against a wall for support. "We have to go," she said, her voice firmer now. "We need to get somewhere safe and regroup."

With Devon's help, Cipher managed to stand, though it was clear they were in considerable pain. "There's a safe house... not far from here," Cipher said through gritted teeth. "We can... regroup there."

Devon nodded, his mind already calculating their next move. They couldn't afford to waste any time. "Let's go."

Together, they made their way out of the control room, moving as quickly as they could given their injuries. The building was eerily silent, the only sounds their labored breathing and the distant hum of the city outside. Devon kept his senses on high alert, every nerve on edge as they navigated the maze of corridors and stairwells.

When they finally emerged into the night air, Devon felt a surge of relief wash over him. They were out, but they weren't safe yet. The streets were empty, but Devon knew that could change at any moment. They needed to keep moving.

They navigated the darkened streets, Cipher leading the way despite their injuries. Devon kept a close eye on Jazz, his heart aching every time she winced or stumbled. But she was strong, and she refused to let the pain slow her down.

When they finally reached the safe house, Devon felt a wave of exhaustion crash over him. The adrenaline that had kept him going was fading, leaving him drained and weary. But they were alive, and they had made it.

Cipher quickly secured the safe house, ensuring they wouldn't be followed. Devon helped Jazz to a chair, his eyes filled with concern as he knelt beside her.

"Let me see your head," Devon said gently, his hands trembling as he examined the cut on her forehead. It wasn't deep, but it had bled a lot, and he wanted to make sure there was no other damage.

Jazz winced as he dabbed at the cut with a clean cloth, but she managed a weak smile. "I'm okay, Dev," she said softly. "It's just a scratch."

Devon's jaw clenched as he focused on cleaning the wound. "You scared the hell out of me, Jazz. I thought I lost you."

Jazz reached up, placing her hand over his. "You didn't lose me. I'm right here."

Devon met her gaze, his heart swelling with love and relief. He leaned in, pressing a gentle kiss to her forehead. "I don't know what I'd do without you."

Jazz's smile widened, and she pulled him into a tight embrace, holding him close as if she never wanted to let go. "You'll never have to find out," she whispered. "We're in this together, remember?"

Devon closed his eyes, savoring the warmth of her embrace. They had been through so much, faced so many dangers, but they had come out the other side together. And as long as they had each other, they could face whatever came next.

After a few moments, Devon reluctantly pulled away, his mind already shifting back to the situation at hand. "We need to figure out our next move," he said, his voice steady. "They'll be looking for us, and we can't stay here for long."

Cipher, who had been sitting quietly in the corner, nodded in agreement. "We need to disappear, at least for a while. Lay low until things cool down. But before we do that, there's something we need to take care of."

Devon raised an eyebrow, his curiosity piqued. "What do you mean?"

Cipher's expression was serious, their eyes sharp. "There's one last piece of the puzzle we need to deal with. The leader we took down—he wasn't the top. There's someone else, someone pulling the strings from the shadows. We need to find them and take them out, or this won't be over."

Jazz frowned, her mind racing as she considered Cipher's words. "How do we find them? We've already crippled their network. They'll be in hiding."

Cipher tapped on their tablet, bringing up a series of encrypted files. "I managed to extract some data before the explosion. It's not much, but it's enough to give us a starting point. We can track their movements, find their safe houses, and flush them out."

Devon felt a surge of determination as he studied the data. They were so close to ending this once and for all. "Then let's do it. We finish what we started."

Jazz nodded, her resolve firm. "We take them down, and then we disappear. For good."

Cipher smiled faintly, their eyes gleaming with a mix of exhaustion and determination. "Let's make sure this time, there's nothing left of them to rebuild."

With their next move decided, the three of them set to work, preparing for the final stage of their mission. The stakes were higher than ever, but they had come too far to turn back now. This was the endgame, and they were ready to see it through to the bitter end.

As they worked, the weight of what they were about to do hung over them like a heavy cloud. But beneath the fear, beneath the exhaustion, there was a sense of purpose—a knowledge that they were fighting for something bigger than themselves. They were fighting for justice, for freedom, and for the chance to finally live the lives they wanted.

And they would stop at nothing to make that happen.

Chapter 13: The Virus of Lust

The next few days passed in a blur of preparation, tension, and sleepless nights. Devon, Jazz, and Cipher worked tirelessly, driven by a shared determination to bring down the last remnants of the shadowy network that had haunted their lives. Every hour was spent analyzing data, planning their next move, and ensuring that every detail was perfect. They knew they were running out of time—their enemies were regrouping, and the window of opportunity was closing fast.

Despite the constant pressure, there was a strange sense of calm that had settled over them. It was the calm that came with knowing the end was in sight, that they were on the verge of finally putting this nightmare behind them. But it was also a dangerous calm, one that threatened to lull them into a false sense of security. Devon was acutely aware of this, and he refused to let his guard down. Not when they were so close to the finish line.

Late one night, as they were poring over the latest intelligence, Cipher looked up from their screen, a frown creasing their brow. "I've found something," they said, their voice tense. "It's a lead, but it's risky."

Jazz leaned in, her eyes narrowing as she studied the data Cipher had pulled up. "What is it?"

"There's a facility on the outskirts of the city," Cipher explained. "It's off the grid—no official records, no digital footprint. But from what I can tell, it's where they've been operating from. If we can get inside, we might be able to find the person who's been pulling the strings. But security is tight. It's a fortress."

Devon's mind raced as he considered their options. The facility was their best shot at finding the leader and ending this once and for all, but it was also a trap waiting to be sprung. "How do we get in?"

Cipher hesitated for a moment before responding. "There's a way, but it's going to require some… creative thinking. They've got the place locked down tight, but there's a backdoor in the system. It's heavily encrypted, but if we can access it, we can shut down their security long enough to get inside."

Jazz looked at Devon, her expression serious. "This is it, Dev. This is our last shot."

Devon nodded; his jaw clenched with determination. "Then we go in, take them out, and finish this."

The plan was set. They would infiltrate the facility, disable the security, and confront the leader. It was a dangerous mission, one that would require all of their skills and wits to pull off. But they had come too far to back down now.

The night before the operation, Devon and Jazz found themselves alone in the safe house, the weight of what was to come pressing down on them. Cipher was in another room, fine-tuning the details of the plan, leaving Devon and Jazz with a rare moment of quiet.

Jazz sat on the edge of the bed; her hands clasped in her lap as she stared at the floor. Her mind was a whirlwind of thoughts—fear, determination, and something else she couldn't quite name. She felt Devon's presence beside her, and when she looked up, she saw the same mix of emotions in his eyes.

"Are you scared?" Devon asked quietly, his voice barely above a whisper.

Jazz nodded, her throat tight. "Yeah. I am. But I know we have to do this."

Devon reached out, taking her hand in his, the warmth of his touch grounding her. "We'll get through this, Jazz. We've made it this far. We can finish this."

Jazz squeezed his hand, drawing strength from his words. "I know. But there's something else, Dev. Something I need to tell you."

Devon's heart skipped a beat as he saw the seriousness in her eyes. "What is it?"

Jazz hesitated, searching for the right words. "I've been thinking a lot about... us. About what happens after all of this is over. I know we've talked about it before, but... I'm scared, Dev. Scared that once this is done, everything will change. That we won't know how to live without the fight."

Devon felt a pang of sadness as he realized she was voicing a fear he had been trying to push down himself. The life they had known—one filled with danger, adrenaline, and constant vigilance—had become their norm. The idea of a life without it, without the fight, was as terrifying as it was appealing.

But he also knew that the life they wanted, the life they had fought so hard for, was within their grasp. "It's going to be different," he admitted, his voice soft. "But different doesn't have to be bad. We'll figure it out together. We'll find a way to live, to be happy. We deserve that, Jazz."

Jazz looked into his eyes, seeing the sincerity and love that had carried them through so much. She felt a warmth spread through her, a sense of peace that she hadn't felt in a long time. "You're right. We do deserve it."

Devon leaned in, capturing her lips in a gentle kiss. It was a kiss that spoke of love, of hope, and of the future they were fighting for. Jazz melted into him; her fears momentarily forgotten as she lost herself in the warmth of his embrace.

As the kiss deepened, the tension that had been building between them for days finally snapped. It was as if all the fear, the uncertainty, and the desire they had been holding back suddenly exploded to the surface. Their kisses became more urgent, more desperate, as they clung to each other, seeking comfort in the only way they knew how.

Devon's hands roamed over her body, his touch both tender and possessive. He could feel the fire between them, the need that had been building since the moment they had first met. It was a need that went beyond lust—it was a need for connection, for reassurance that they were still alive, still together.

Jazz responded with equal intensity, her hands tangling in his hair as she pressed herself against him. She could feel the heat of his body, the strength in his arms, and it drove her wild. In that moment, nothing else mattered. Not the mission, not the danger—only the two of them, here and now.

They fell back onto the bed, their bodies entwined as they gave in to the passion that had been simmering beneath the surface for so long. The air around them was charged with desire, a raw, unfiltered need that consumed them both. It was a moment of pure, unadulterated emotion, a release of everything they had been holding back.

As they moved together, their breaths coming in ragged gasps, Devon felt a sense of urgency, as if this might be the last time they would ever have this—this connection, this love. He poured everything he had into that moment, wanting to show Jazz just how much she meant to him, how much he needed her.

Jazz felt the same urgency, the same need to hold on to him, to this, as if it might slip away at any moment. She matched his intensity, her hands and lips exploring every inch of him, memorizing the feel of his skin, the sound of his voice, the way he made her feel alive.

Their movements became more frantic, more desperate, as they neared the edge. It was a rush of sensations—heat, pleasure, love—all wrapped up in a whirlwind of emotion that threatened to overwhelm them both.

And then, finally, they found release, their bodies shuddering as they collapsed into each other, spent and breathless. The room was filled with the sound of their breathing, the silence that followed heavy with the weight of what they had just shared.

Devon held Jazz close, his heart pounding in his chest as he tried to catch his breath. He could feel her trembling in his arms, her face buried in his neck as she clung to him. He knew that this moment was about more than just physical desire—it was about the need to feel connected, to remind themselves that they were still alive, still together.

"I love you, Jazz," Devon whispered, his voice rough with emotion. "I love you so much."

Jazz tightened her hold on him, her own voice choked with tears. "I love you too, Dev. I'll always love you."

They lay there in silence, their bodies entwined, as the world outside continued to turn. In that moment, nothing else mattered—only the love they shared, and the promise of a future they were determined to fight for.

But as the night wore on, and the reality of what was to come began to seep back in, they knew that this moment of peace was fleeting. The mission still loomed ahead of them, the danger still very real. And as much as they wanted to stay in each other's arms forever, they couldn't afford to let their guard down.

They eventually pulled themselves from the bed, their movements slow and reluctant as they prepared for the day ahead. There was no need for words—everything that needed to be said had been said in the silence of their embrace. They knew what they were fighting for, and they knew they would face it together.

As they dressed and armed themselves, the tension that had momentarily been forgotten began to creep back in. But it was a different kind of tension now—a tension born of determination, of resolve. They were ready.

When they finally emerged from the room, Cipher was waiting for them, their expression unreadable. But there was a hint of something in their eyes—approval, perhaps, or understanding. "It's time," Cipher said, their voice calm and steady.

Chapter 14: Rebooting Romance

Devon and Jazz nodded in unison, a shared understanding passing between them as they steeled themselves for the final confrontation. The atmosphere in the room was thick with anticipation, the kind that could either sharpen or unravel the nerves. But after everything they had been through, Devon knew that nothing could shake their resolve. They had made it this far, and they weren't about to back down now.

Cipher led them through a series of last-minute checks, ensuring that every detail of their plan was in place. Devon watched as the hacker's fingers danced over the keyboard, inputting commands with the kind of precision that came from years of experience. The room was filled with the soft hum of electronics, punctuated by the occasional beep of a confirmation message.

"We're ready," Cipher finally said, their voice breaking the silence. "The system's backdoor is primed. Once we're in, we'll have a narrow window to shut down their defenses. We can't afford any mistakes."

Devon nodded; his mind laser-focused on the task ahead. "We won't make any."

Jazz stood beside him, her expression a mix of determination and calm. Despite the tension, there was a newfound clarity in her eyes—a sense of purpose that seemed to radiate from her. Devon could see the transformation she had undergone since they first started this journey together. She was no longer just fighting for survival; she was fighting for a future they could both believe in.

They moved out with the kind of efficiency that had become second nature. The city was dark and quiet, a stark contrast to the storm of emotions swirling within each of them. They navigated the streets in silence, their every movement calculated to avoid detection. The facility they were targeting was heavily guarded, and they couldn't afford to make a single misstep.

As they approached the facility's perimeter, Cipher tapped into the security network, overriding the external cameras and sensors. Devon marveled at the hacker's skill—it was like watching a maestro conduct an intricate symphony, each note carefully placed to ensure success.

"We're in," Cipher whispered, nodding for Devon and Jazz to move forward. "Stay close and follow my lead."

Devon's heart pounded in his chest as they slipped through the facility's defenses. The adrenaline coursing through his veins was a familiar rush, but this time it was tinged with a sense of finality. This was their last stand, and everything hinged on their ability to outmaneuver their enemies.

They crept through the facility, the darkness their only ally as they made their way deeper into the heart of the operation. The walls were lined with servers, blinking lights indicating the flow of information through the network. It was the nerve center of their enemies' operations, and Devon knew that once they took it down, there would be no coming back.

But just as they reached the control room, a sudden noise shattered the silence—a metallic clatter, followed by the unmistakable sound of footsteps approaching. Devon's blood ran cold as he realized they had been discovered.

"Get ready," Devon hissed, his voice low but urgent. He could feel Jazz tensing beside him, her hand steady as she gripped her weapon.

The footsteps grew louder, closer, until the door to the control room swung open and a group of armed guards stormed in. Devon and Jazz reacted instantly, their training kicking in as they engaged the intruders in a fierce, close-quarters battle.

The room erupted in chaos, the air filled with the deafening sound of gunfire and the acrid smell of smoke. Devon moved with lethal precision; his every movement calculated to neutralize the threat. Beside him, Jazz was a whirlwind of controlled fury, her strikes swift and deadly.

Cipher stayed focused on the task at hand, fingers flying over the keyboard as they worked to shut down the facility's systems. The hacker's calm under pressure was astonishing, a testament to their years of experience in high-stakes operations.

As the last of the guards fell, Devon and Jazz quickly scanned the room, ensuring there were no remaining threats. The adrenaline was still pumping through their veins, but they couldn't afford to let their guard down—not yet.

Cipher's voice cut through the haze of battle. "I've almost got it. Just a few more seconds…"

But before Cipher could finish, the door to the control room opened again, and this time, it wasn't more guards—it was him. The man they had been hunting, the one who had orchestrated the entire operation from the shadows. He stood in the doorway, a cold, calculating smile on his face as he surveyed the scene.

"So, you've made it this far," the man said, his voice smooth and unruffled. "I must admit, I didn't expect you to survive the explosion. But it seems I underestimated you."

Devon's grip on his weapon tightened as he stared at the man who had caused so much pain, so much destruction. This was the moment they had been waiting for, the moment when they could finally end it all. But the man's calm demeanor unnerved him—there was something off, something that didn't sit right.

"What's your plan?" the man continued, stepping further into the room. "Take me down, destroy the network, and then what? Do you really think you can just walk away? That the people I work for will let you live out your happy little lives in peace?"

Jazz's eyes narrowed as she took a step forward, her voice cold as ice. "We're going to end this. And if that means taking you down, so be it."

The man chuckled, a dark, mocking sound that sent chills down Devon's spine. "Oh, you're welcome to try. But I think you'll find that I'm not so easily defeated."

Before Devon or Jazz could react, the man reached into his pocket and pulled out a small, sleek device. Devon's heart sank as he realized what it was—another detonator.

"I've rigged the entire facility," the man said, his smile widening. "One press of this button, and everything goes up in flames. Including you."

Devon's mind raced as he tried to calculate their options. They had come so far, fought so hard, but now they were faced with the possibility of losing it all in an instant.

"Put it down," Devon said, his voice steady despite the fear gnawing at him. "You don't have to do this."

The man's eyes gleamed with malice as he shook his head. "Oh, but I do. You see, I can't afford to let you walk away. You've seen too much, learned too much. And if I can't have this operation, then no one will."

For a split second, time seemed to stand still. Devon's mind raced, his instincts screaming at him to do something, anything, to stop the man before it was too late. But in that moment of hesitation, the man's thumb moved toward the detonator, and Devon knew he was out of time.

But before the man could press the button, a shot rang out, echoing through the control room. Devon's eyes widened in shock as he saw the man stagger backward, the detonator slipping from his grasp as he clutched his chest.

Jazz stood beside Devon, her weapon still raised, her eyes blazing with fury. The shot had been clean, precise—a single bullet that had struck the man squarely in the chest.

The man's eyes widened in surprise as he crumpled to the ground, blood pooling around him. He gasped for breath, his eyes locking onto Jazz's as he realized what had just happened.

"You... you won't... get away with this," he choked out, his voice barely a whisper. "They'll come for you... they'll find you..."

Jazz's expression was cold, unyielding. "Let them try."

With that, the man's eyes closed, and his body went limp. The detonator lay on the floor beside him, harmless and unused.

For a moment, there was nothing but silence. Devon's heart pounded in his chest as he processed what had just happened. They had done it—they had taken down the man who had been pulling the strings, the one who had orchestrated the entire operation. But the cost had been high, and the danger was far from over.

Cipher's voice broke the silence, calm and composed. "The network is down. The operation is finished."

Devon looked over at Cipher, then back at Jazz, who was still staring at the man's lifeless body. He could see the toll it had taken on her, the weight of what she had just done. But there was also a sense of relief, of closure. They had finished what they had started.

"We need to get out of here," Devon said, his voice firm. "Before anyone else shows up."

Jazz nodded, her expression softening as she turned to him. "Yeah. Let's go."

They left the control room in silence, the weight of their victory heavy on their shoulders. The facility was eerily quiet, the once-bustling nerve center now a tomb for the operation they had destroyed.

As they made their way out of the facility, Devon couldn't help but think about what the man had said—that their enemies wouldn't stop, that they would come after them. He knew there was truth in those words, but he also knew that they had come too far to turn back now.

When they finally stepped out into the night air, Devon felt a sense of relief wash over him. They were out, they were alive, and they had won. But as he looked at Jazz, he could see the exhaustion in her eyes, the weight of everything they had been through.

He reached out, taking her hand in his, and gave it a reassuring squeeze. "It's over, Jazz. We did it!!

Chapter 15: The Encryption of Freedom

Devon squeezed Jazz's hand, his voice full of emotion as he repeated, "We did it, Jazz. It's over."

Jazz looked at him, her eyes reflecting a mixture of relief, exhaustion, and something deeper—a hope that had been buried for so long but was now beginning to resurface. She took a deep breath, the cool night air filling her lungs, and for the first time in what felt like forever, she allowed herself to believe that they had truly made it to the other side.

"It's really over," she whispered, as if saying it aloud would make it more real.

Devon nodded, pulling her into his arms. "Yes, it is. And now we can finally start living."

They stood there for a moment, holding each other in the darkness, the world around them feeling strangely quiet and still. The battles, the chases, the constant danger—they were all behind them now. The weight that had pressed down on them for so long had finally lifted, leaving them both feeling lighter, freer than they had in years.

But even as they embraced, Devon knew that their journey wasn't entirely over. The man they had just taken down had hinted at a larger threat, a network of powerful people who wouldn't take kindly to what they had done. There were still loose ends to tie up, and they couldn't afford to let their guard down completely—not yet.

"We should get out of here," Devon said softly, pulling back just enough to look into Jazz's eyes. "We can't stay too long in one place, not until we're sure they've stopped looking for us."

Jazz nodded, her mind already shifting back to practical matters. "Cipher, do you have a plan for where we go next?"

Cipher, who had been standing a few paces away, watching their exchange with a hint of something like pride, stepped forward. "I've been monitoring the situation. There's a safe route out of the city, one they won't expect us to take. From there, we'll go dark—change our identities, our appearances, everything. It'll be like we never existed."

Jazz exchanged a glance with Devon, and he could see the relief in her eyes. It was a drastic measure, but it was what they needed to finally put this life behind them and start anew.

"Let's do it," Devon said, his voice filled with determination. "The sooner we disappear, the better."

They moved quickly, following Cipher's lead as they navigated the backstreets of the city. The tension in the air was palpable, but it was different from before—more controlled, more focused. They were no longer running from something; they were running toward something—toward a future that was finally within their grasp.

The route Cipher had planned was clever, taking them through a series of underground tunnels and abandoned buildings that kept them off the grid and away from any prying eyes. Devon couldn't help but admire the hacker's ingenuity; every step was calculated, every move designed to keep them safe.

After what felt like hours, they emerged from the final tunnel into the outskirts of the city. The landscape had shifted from urban sprawl to something quieter, more rural. The stars shone brightly overhead, and for the first time in a long while, Devon felt a sense of peace.

Cipher had arranged for a car to be waiting for them, parked in a secluded spot where it was unlikely to be noticed. As they approached, Devon felt a mixture of relief and anticipation. This was it—the final step before they could truly disappear.

"Here's how it's going to work," Cipher said, turning to face them. "I'll drive you to a safe location where we can set up new identities. We'll leave behind everything that could trace back to us—phones, devices, anything with a digital footprint. Once we're settled, you'll be free to start over."

Devon and Jazz nodded, understanding the gravity of what Cipher was saying. They were about to erase their old lives, to become entirely new people. It was both terrifying and exhilarating.

As they got into the car, Devon reached out and took Jazz's hand, giving it a reassuring squeeze. "No matter what happens next, we'll face it together," he said, his voice filled with love and determination.

Jazz smiled at him, a warmth spreading through her chest. "Together," she agreed.

The car ride was mostly silent, each of them lost in their thoughts as they sped through the night. Cipher drove with the kind of focus that came from years of experience, navigating the roads with ease as they put more and more distance between themselves and the city.

After what felt like hours, they finally arrived at a small, secluded cabin deep in the woods. It was the kind of place that was off the map, hidden from the world—a perfect location for them to regroup and plan their next steps.

Cipher parked the car and turned to face them. "This is it. We'll stay here for a few days while I finalize the details of your new identities. After that, you'll be free to go wherever you want. I'll make sure the world thinks you've disappeared."

Devon and Jazz exchanged a look, the enormity of what was about to happen settling over them. This was the beginning of their new lives, and while it was daunting, it was also the chance they had been fighting for.

"Thank you, Cipher," Jazz said, her voice filled with genuine gratitude. "We couldn't have done this without you."

Cipher nodded, their expression softening for a moment. "You two have been through a lot. You deserve a chance to start over."

They spent the next few days in the cabin, going over the details of their new identities and preparing for the final step in their plan. Devon and Jazz used the time to rest, to reflect on everything that had happened, and to plan for the future they wanted to build together.

On the last night before they were set to leave, Devon and Jazz sat together on the porch of the cabin, the stars twinkling overhead as a cool breeze rustled the leaves around them. It was a peaceful, almost surreal moment, one that felt like a dream after everything they had been through.

"I can't believe it's really over," Jazz said softly, leaning her head on Devon's shoulder. "We're actually free."

Devon wrapped his arm around her, pulling her close. "We are. And now we get to build the life we've always wanted."

Jazz smiled, a sense of contentment washing over her. "What do you think we should do? Where should we go?"

Devon thought for a moment, considering their options. "Anywhere we want. Maybe somewhere quiet, where we can start fresh. I've always liked the idea of a small town, somewhere near the ocean."

Jazz closed her eyes, imagining the life they could have—a life filled with peace, love, and the simple joys they had been denied for so long. "That sounds perfect."

They sat in silence for a while, savoring the moment, the future stretching out before them like an open road. There was no more fear, no more running—only the promise of a new beginning.

When they finally went back inside, they found Cipher waiting for them, the details of their new identities finalized and ready. It was time to say goodbye to the people they had been and embrace the people they were about to become.

As they packed their few belongings and prepared to leave, Devon and Jazz shared one last look, a silent promise passing between them. They had faced so much together, overcome so many obstacles, and now they were ready to start the next chapter of their lives.

As they drove away from the cabin, leaving their old lives behind, Devon felt a sense of peace he hadn't known in years. He had Jazz by his side, and together, they were unstoppable.

They didn't know what the future held, but they knew they would face it together—no matter where the road took them.

And as they drove into the horizon, the past finally behind them, they knew one thing for certain: they had earned their freedom, and they were going to live every moment of it to the fullest.

THE END